You Can't Take Twenty Dogs on a Date

Westminster Press Books
by
BETTY CAVANNA

You Can't Take
    Twenty Dogs on a Date

Catchpenny Street

Petey

Going on Sixteen

A Touch of Magic

6 on Easy Street

Love, Laurie

Lasso Your Heart

Two's Company

Spring Comes Riding

Paintbox Summer

A Girl Can Dream

Spurs for Suzanna

The Black Spaniel Mystery

You Can't Take Twenty Dogs on a Date

By
BETTY CAVANNA

F- Cav

~~98~~

141

THE WESTMINSTER PRESS
Philadelphia

Book Design by Dorothy Alden Smith

Published by The Westminster Press®
Philadelphia, Pennsylvania

PRINTED IN THE UNITED STATES OF AMERICA

Library of Congress Cataloging in Publication Data

Cavanna, Betty, 1909–
　　You can't take twenty dogs on a date.

　　Editions for 1949 and 1954 published under title: She's my girl!
　　SUMMARY: When Jo is forced to give up her plans for college, she opens a boarding kennel for dogs.
　　[1. Dogs—Fiction]　I. Title.
PZ7. C286Yo　　[Fic]　　77–432
ISBN 0-664-32613-7

1

BRETT'S PHARMACY was the teen hangout. Almost every summer afternoon the stools at the long counter were filled with girls and boys in sawed-off jeans.

Jo Redmond and Ginny Clark felt that they were really getting a little too sophisticated to rub elbows with the high school crowd, but dropping in at Brett's for soft drinks had become a habit. And the presence of Stephen Chance behind the counter was a new attraction few of the older girls could resist.

That afternoon, Jo followed Ginny a little reluctantly into the drugstore. She had had a few dates with Steve, but she didn't plan to join the ranks of his admirers. "A boy that sought after is likely to be spoiled," Mrs. Redmond said.

Jo didn't quite agree with her mother, yet she understood what she meant. Steve seemed to relish the fact that he had a way with girls.

All the counter stools were filled, but there was an empty booth at the rear, and Ginny scurried for it. Jo slid along the bench opposite, facing away from the door.

The fewer people she had to talk to, the better. "I think I'll go overboard and have a chocolate fudge sundae," she said.

Ginny was beckoning to someone coming through the door, and a minute later Nancy Valentine joined them. "Hello, Jo. Room for me?"

"Plenty!" Jo moved over and Nancy sat down. She was a small, self-contained girl with eyes speckled like a robin's egg and brown hair worn straight and long. A much more striking combination than my brown eyes and almost-red hair, Jo thought.

"What's new?"

"Plenty!" Ginny repeated Jo's reply deliberately, meeting her eyes across the table. "Or is it a secret?"

"It's no secret," Jo said, though she would have preferred to let the news seep rather than surge. "Ginny and I had planned to room together at college, you know. But I'm not going to be able to go, that's all."

"Oh, Jo, what a shame! With your grades and everything."

Jo glanced around, hoping nobody would overhear. "There will be other years," she said without much conviction. Then, as she saw Steve, spruce in a starched white jacket, coming across the store toward them, she hurried on.

"What Ginny's really bothered by is who she may draw for a roommate. Remember Lisa Bowen, the first year she went to George School?" Anything to get the subject off herself.

Nancy shook her head.

"She was assigned to the daughter of a hotelkeeper from Asbury Park, two hundred pounds of her," Jo teased. "With about five pounds of cookies and candy delivered each week."

Nancy laughed, but Ginny groaned. "Suppose something like that happens to me! You know how I gain if I even look at anything fattening."

"Now watch her order a banana split," said Steve, standing above them.

"A small lemon Coke," said Ginny deliberately.

"There's a girl who can change her mind just like that!" Steve snapped his fingers.

Jo and Nancy both laughed as they gave their orders, then went back to the conversation. "I wouldn't worry too much," Nancy comforted Ginny. "If you draw somebody too dreadful, you can make a change."

"But all our plans!" Ginny was feeling worse by the moment. She looked at Jo. "Our bedspreads and lamps and everything." Then she turned contrite. "I'm sorry! I know it's much worse for you than it is for me, but I am devastated." Her blue eyes were eloquent.

Jo was swept by the odd sensation of being years older than the girl opposite her. "I guess we're growing up, Ginny," she said gently. "I guess it's too much to hope to always get the breaks." She broke off abruptly as Steve returned with a laden tray, balanced precariously but professionally on one hand.

"How'm I doin'?" he asked.

"You're doing fine!" Nancy told him. "Attracting quite a gallery too." She nodded toward the counter.

Nancy had a way of kidding people that made them like it. "Ah, but you should see me in the delivery van. Shouldn't she, Jo?"

"Some van!" To the girls Jo said, "It's a VW Rabbit."

Nancy measured Steve's six-feet-two with amusement sparkling in her eyes. "It can't be done."

Jo sat back and listened to the continuing conversation. Steve likes feminine girls, she thought. When Nancy or Ginny is around, he scarcely notices me. She wished she had her companions' knack for small talk. She wished she were five-foot-two, instead of five-seven.

Then she found Steve looking at her. "Struck dumb by our witty repartee, Jo?"

"I guess today just isn't my day," she confessed.

"How about tomorrow? I'll stop by."

He still liked her then, wanted to see her. Or was he teasing? She couldn't tell.

After Steve had left, Ginny shook her head in mock despair. "How do you do it, Josie? You don't say boo, and you're the girl he goes for. What's the technique?"

"I haven't any technique," Jo said honestly. "And you know Steve. A new girl every month! My time's about up." She smiled and shrugged.

Later, however, riding home from Ginny's with her bicycle basket full of groceries, she wondered whether she would be able to say good-by as casually as she pretended. She liked Steve Chance. He was sometimes irritating, but he was also stimulating. He had a keen mind, when he wanted to be serious—which was seldom. She felt that she hadn't even scratched the surface of his personality, which she suspected might be quite complex.

A car, about to pass her, honked and pulled over to the side of the road. Jo braked, slid down off the seat of her bike, and looked back to recognize Dr. Luke Webster, the local veterinarian, one of her father's close friends.

"Hi, Uncle Doc! I didn't recognize your car." Jo turned and crossed the road, bringing her wheel close to the driver's side.

Dr. Webster leaned out the window. "I just pulled out of your place. Not a soul home. The folks left already?"

It was a relief to talk to someone who already knew about her father's illness. Jo didn't feel up to making an explanation one more time that day. "They got off this morning. Dad wanted me to call you tonight after office hours to let you know."

"No use putting it off," Dr. Webster said. His eyes were both kindly and searching as he looked at Jo. "Anything I can do for you?"

"Not a thing." Jo had trouble keeping her voice even. She was smitten by the sudden feeling that she could burst into tears without any trouble at all.

The doctor rescued her by not noticing. "I'm going to miss your pop when I have to do an emergency operation," he said with a shake of his head. "I could always give him an SOS."

"I'll be right here all summer. And I'm not too squeamish, Uncle Doc."

Dr. Webster considered Jo speculatively. "I may take you up on that."

9

"I wish you would." Jo was sincere.

"Sure you wouldn't keel over on me?"

"I don't think so."

"Okay. It's a deal. If I get in a jam, I'll give you a ring."

Jo nodded, pleased. She liked to be around Uncle Doc and his dogs. There was so much to see, so much to learn. Every minute she had ever spent in his office had been fascinating.

"Josie." Luke Webster's voice changed abruptly, taking on a note of tenderness. "There's something I've been wanting to tell you. I'm sorry I couldn't save Inky. I did my level best."

"Oh, I know you did!" Tears stung Jo's eyelids. "I'm sorry. I still can't talk about it. We—we all thought she was a pretty exceptional pup."

"She was," Dr. Webster agreed. "She had spirit and personality, and it was just a darned unfortunate accident. A few months more and she'd have developed enough sense not to dash into the road without looking. You couldn't blame the driver of the car that hit her, Jo."

"No," Jo admitted, without meeting his eyes.

"You know there's only one way to get over losing a dog, child."

"What's that?"

"Get another. And that's my advice to you."

Get another dog now? Jo considered Uncle Doc's prescription as she rode on home. But no other dog would be the same. And besides, food for a dog would cost money. Instead of considering getting another dog, she should be thinking about getting a job.

The possibility had occurred to Jo more than once in

10

the days since her father had been taken ill. But she didn't know quite where to turn, and she had no special skills, like typing or shorthand. Still, Steve had his drugstore job and Chuck Trimble was working at the supermarket. If they could find summer work, maybe she could too.

Reaching the lane, Jo got down and pushed her bicycle up the short rise of ground toward the house. A strange sound from the rear of the garage made her stop and listen. For a moment she thought it was an animal in pain.

Then Ricky's red head appeared around the corner. He was leaping in the air with a peculiar, two-legged gallop, and at intervals he stopped to paw the ground and neigh. Attached, somehow, to the seat of his jeans, was a brush made of long fronds of privet, undoubtedly meant to be a horse's tail. Toby Apple followed him within a few paces, engaged in the same remarkable antics, to which he had added one embellishment. Every now and then he reached back with one hand and switched his tail realistically, while hedge leaves showered all around.

Jo stood and watched the two nine-year-olds until they disappeared once more behind the garage, completely unaware that they had an audience. It wasn't until she started to walk on toward the garage that she noticed the top of the hedge. No more than two feet had been cut —just enough to provide fronds for the horses' tails. And as Ricky's enthusiasm had apparently waned, his clippers had risen, because the two feet were trimmed on a sharp upward angle.

"Ricky Redmond!" Jo called.

She was answered by a distant neigh.

"Ricky!" Jo parked her bicycle and started toward the

11

break in the hedge. She knew perfectly well where the boys had gone—to the abandoned kennels where the former owner of the Redmond house had bred boxers. Weed-grown now, and out of repair, the big exercise pen was used by Ricky and Toby for a make-believe corral.

Keeping her amusement under control, Jo marched firmly down the path between the kennel runs and pushed open the rusted wire gate to the exercise yard. Sure enough, in the far corner Ricky and Toby were standing, a bucket of water between them, each taking turns drinking by ducking their heads into the pail and lapping up water with their tongues.

Toby saw Jo first. "You can't come in here," he called.

"Sh!" Ricky told him. "We're horses. We can't talk."

Jo stood with her hands on her hips and shook her head. "You are completely incredible."

Ricky responded with a noise between a neigh and a bray.

Toby, less intent than Ricky, felt called upon to explain. "I'm King of the Wind and Ricky's Thunderhead."

Jo's hands remained on her hips. "Oh, he is!" Her gaze shifted to her brother. "Well, my four-footed friend, suppose you explain what happened to the job you were going to do on the hedge. I gather you've been off in Wyoming all afternoon and haven't had time to give it a second thought?"

Ricky stopped being a horse and stood upright, frowning. "Oh, now, Jo!"

"Don't 'oh, now, Jo' me!"

"But—"

"We made a bargain," Jo said firmly. "And you've got

12

to keep your end of it. You get half done today and I'll do the rest tomorrow." She squinted at the sky. "You'll have a couple of good hours yet."

"Hours?" Ricky's voice rose to a wail. "Hours?" His tail dragged disconsolately along the ground as he came toward his sister. "I thought in about fifteen minutes it was going to be time to eat!"

Jo stood with her back against the gate so that Ricky could go through ahead of her. Toby, looking abashed, followed hard on his heels. Jo winked at Toby, and grinned to show she bore no malice—that she was just trying to see that Ricky stuck to his deal. But Toby, resentful of all older sisters, would not smile back at her. He joined his friend, who was still grumbling under his breath, and walked with him toward the offending hedge that screened the kennels from the house.

Jo followed the boys slowly. She began to wish she had been less abrupt. The trampled grass of the path and of the make-believe corral testified to the fun the two boys had been having. What the place really needs, Jo thought in passing, is a scythe to hack down the briers and weeds.

For the first time in the four years her family had lived on the old MacNeill property, Jo turned and really looked at the kennels. They seemed well constructed, and still quite sound of roof. Uncle Doc had said once that it was a shame not to use them, and Jo had been entertaining a vague idea of someday breeding Inky—but that was in the past. Jo ran a finger along the wire fencing and counted the pens. Ten on one side of the path, ten on the other, each big enough to lodge a full-grown boxer. Mr. MacNeill must have put quite a good deal of money into

13

his hobby of breeding dogs.

Like her mother, Jo hated waste, and the abandoned kennels had always vaguely disturbed her. Now they seemed a positive blot on the landscape, neglected and rundown and empty. The setting sun lighted them with a merciless glow, and a tendril of honeysuckle that had climbed the wire fencing waved forlornly in the light June breeze.

Walking thoughtfully back to her bicycle, Jo wheeled it into the garage and took the groceries from the wicker basket. Then, after a brief glance at Ricky, who had gone back to work on the hedge, she went up the steps of the house and through the kitchen door.

There was dinner to get and, as a peace offering, she supposed she might ask Toby to stay and eat with them. But a new idea crowded the thought from Jo's mind. She stood, the groceries still in their brown paper bags, looking out the kitchen window at nothing. Was it a crazy notion, or might it work? Should she phone Uncle Doc and suggest it, just for fun? Would her mother approve, or would she veto it as impractical? Jo began to wish that Ricky were a few years older. Then they could go into this thing on a partnership basis.

Aloud she said, "Why not?"

2

LEANING BACK, his elbows on the top step of the Redmonds' side porch, Steve Chance looked up at a high-flying June moon. Jo sat two steps below him, her knees gathered into her arms, and wondered whether she should tell him about her idea, which had come from seed to bud overnight.

Bubbling with the urge to talk about it, Jo had repeatedly tried to reach Uncle Doc. First she had been told that he was busy operating, then that he had been called out of town for the day. Ricky was too full of his own concerns to make a good listener, and until Steve had stopped by on his way home from the drugstore, there hadn't been another soul around all day.

"Steve." Jo turned her head and glanced upward.

"Uh-huh?" Steve leaned back still farther, and yawned companionably.

"I've been thinking I ought to get something to do this summer—like a job."

Steve thought for a minute. "Golly," he said, "it's too bad you're not a boy. Fella asked me if I wanted to work

15

in a gas station just today. But I like the drugstore fine."

"Girls work in gas stations," murmured Jo.

Steve grunted. "Oh, sure, but not girls like you."

His tone of voice amused Jo. "Typical male chauvinist!" She chuckled and said, "Can you think of anything else I might do?"

After a pause Steve said, "Well, heck, there ought to be something. Can you type?"

Jo shook her head. "The straight academic course, that's me."

"Well, you could baby-sit, maybe."

"Yes, but the work is spotty, and there's not that much money in it."

"Is money so important?" Steve asked.

"This summer, yes."

The boy nodded reflectively. "Sure. I'm a dope. I forgot your dad and all."

"Steve—" Why was it so hard to come right out with it? Jo wondered.

"What's on your mind?" Steve uncrossed his legs, slid down two steps, and leaned forward.

"I've got an idea."

"You don't say?"

Jo ignored his teasing. "It's sort of crazy, but I think it would work. Steve, how do you think it would be if I were to open a summer boarding kennel? D'you think I could get any dogs?"

"A boarding kennel?" Steve pulled himself upright. "Here?"

Jo nodded. "We have the old MacNeill runs, you know, behind the hedge. It wouldn't be too hard to fix them up again, and I'd have Uncle Doc to call on if I got in a jam." Suddenly the thoughts that had been tumbling in her mind all day poured out in a rush. "I like dogs, you know, I always have. And, generally, dogs like me. Besides, I could be right home here with Mother. She's going to be on the lonely side this summer with Dad away."

"But a boarding kennel! Good grief, Jo, that isn't a girl's job."

"Why not?" Jo bridled.

Steve frowned. "Well, heck, I should think you could see. You'd need a hired man, or at least a boy, to clean out the runs, and all."

Jo had expected opposition. "Ricky could help."

"Ricky!" Steve's snort was descriptive. "He's just a little kid."

"Well, you'll admit it's a good idea," Jo persisted, though she felt rather deflated. "I mean, with the runs here and all. And Uncle Doc was telling Dad just the other night how crowded all the boarding kennels get in the summer. There just isn't enough space to supply the vacation demand."

"Vacation demand—what are you talking about?"

"People who go away on summer vacations generally park their dogs. You know that, Steve!" Jo's voice had an edge to it, because she felt she was being put down.

"So you want to take on their headaches? Suppose some dogs get sick?"

"There's Uncle Doc."

"Or run away?"

"They can't run away if they're penned up."

17

Steve scratched the back of his neck and moaned. "It's a lousy idea, Jo. Skip it. Say you got a dozen dogs. They'd bark all night. They'd have fleas and ticks. They'd have to be bathed and dipped and fed." He shook his head. "Can you see your mother letting you turn her kitchen into a horsemeat cafeteria?"

Steve had touched on a point that Jo had been dodging. "You're not only a male chauvinist, you're a wet blanket," she said.

"It's just not a girl's job, that's all."

"A girl's job!" Jo mimicked. "Move into the twentieth century, Steve!"

Her very annoyance seemed to reassure Steve. He leaned back again and looked up at the moon. Softly he began to whistle:

"I can do anything you can do better
I can do anything better than you!"

Jo could fit the words to the tune, and she knew Steve was waiting for her to come through with the next line, but she kept quiet and sat tapping her foot against the riser of the step until he finished.

"I think you're mean," she said finally, then felt childish for allowing herself to be baited.

Steve shifted to a more comfortable position. "And I think you're impractical. Just be glad you have me around to advise you, Josie. First thing you know, if it weren't for me, you'd be sweeping out kennels in a man's old felt hat, just like that dog woman."

Jo knew immediately that he was thinking of Mrs. Truck, who had been in the dog-raising business for as many years as Jo could remember. Winter and summer,

18

she always looked the same. Wispy hair sprayed from under a stained and battered hat. Her high-laced boots had run-over heels, and a man's khaki trousers were supported by a tooled leather belt of dubious Western origin. Mrs. Truck!

"There's no point to making it all sound completely repulsive!" Jo flared.

"It is repulsive," Steve said calmly.

"It isn't!"

Steve shrugged. "Have it your own way." He stood up and yawned. "I've got to be ambling." Reaching out, he patted Jo lightly on the head.

Afterward, Jo knew that this was the moment at which she could have avoided an out-and-out quarrel. She liked Steve. She didn't want to antagonize him, even if he failed to share her enthusiasm for the dog business. Yet she twisted away from the patronizing gesture and stood up, her chin high and in her eyes no invitation to stay longer.

"Bye now."

"Bye."

It wasn't the words they said. It was the way they said them. Steve, hands in his pockets, went whistling toward his car, and Jo went into the house without waiting for him to drive down the lane. She banged the screen door and muttered, "Antiquated, that's what he is. Putting a girl down!" She stood in the middle of the living room, her eyes stormy, her chin thrust forward, until the car reached the road and the sound of its motor died on the night air.

Then she selected a magazine from the pile on the coffee table and went up to bed. Ricky was already in his room, working on a rocket model, with his radio blaring away.

"Turn that thing down, Ricky," Jo called. "Please!" She felt less indignant now, just irritable and sulky, and as she undressed, she looked in the mirror and made a face at her image. "Mrs. Truck!" The girl who looked back, with creamy skin and smooth long hair caught back by a leather barrette, hardly looked like Mrs. Truck!

Propped up in bed with two pillows under her head, Jo opened the magazine, but she didn't read. Her glance wandered restlessly around the familiar room, furnished with pine from the Pennsylvania Dutch country, and curtained in red-and-yellow-sprigged calico. It was a cheerful room, and she loved it, but tonight it made her feel hemmed in.

After a while she called good night to Ricky, closed her door, and turned out her light. Then, for a long time, she stood by the back window and looked out on the deserted kennels silhouetted by the thin light of the moon. She could imagine them repaired and painted and filled with dogs—all sorts of dogs, big and little and old and young. And in spite of anything Steve Chance might say, she still thought it would be fun to take care of them. She wasn't going to give up, not until she had had a chance to talk to Uncle Doc.

But when Jo approached the veterinarian the next morning it was without the certainty she would have had if Steve had not been so scornful of her scheme. She outlined her idea tentatively, sitting on the corner of the battered old desk that occupied an alcove in the consult-

20

ing room, and she wasn't especially surprised when Uncle Doc's first reaction was much like Steve's.

"It's a pretty big order for a girl."

"But there's a need for a summer boarding kennel around these parts?"

"You bet!" On this point the doctor was not hesitant. "I've got my place booked solid now till September, and people keep calling up in a tizzy, because the same thing's true everywhere else."

"See?" Jo was faintly triumphant.

Dr. Webster pulled his right ear thoughtfully. "You'd aim to go into this alone, with only Ricky to fetch and carry for you?"

"I want to make some money," Jo said honestly. "Would a kennel pay if I should hire help?"

"Nope, don't s'pose it would. Gosh, Josie, if you were only a boy."

"If I were only a boy, what?"

"Well, the way I figure," said Dr. Webster, leaning back against his examining table, "a man can take care of up to thirty dogs. Assuming an average charge of five dollars a day per dog, with half the gross going into food, supplies, advertising and maintenance, there's a nice little business for you. But a girl—?"

Jo hadn't quite followed Uncle Doc's mathematical juggling, but she did recognize that he was getting interested. "Suppose I only counted on between ten and twenty dogs? There are only twenty kennel runs, anyway. Couldn't a girl handle twenty dogs?"

Dr. Webster frowned. "Twenty dogs is a lot of dawg."

Jo smiled. "Of course I couldn't consider it, if it weren't for you, Uncle Doc. But having you so close, in an emergency—"

"Oh, sure, sure." This angle of the proposition didn't bother the vet. It was the day-in, day-out drudgery he questioned. "Tell you what I'll do," he finally proposed. "I'll stop by after lunch and take a look at those runs. If they need much money spent on them, you'd better forget the whole proposition, Jo. But if they should be usable—well, we'll see."

On the way home from Dr. Webster's office, Jo stopped at the library and picked up three books, one on how to raise dogs, one on feeding, and one on dogs as a business. The latter had a chapter on "The Boarding Kennel," and this Jo read with keen interest but increasing astonishment.

She hadn't realized there were so many hazards, and so many details, involved. Sentences leaped up from the printed page to dance in her head. "Attendants should always be cautioned to back out of pens. . . . Flies are worse pests in kennels than is often realized; they attack the prick ear at its tip, drop ears on the fold near the skull. . . . For dogs that play with their drinking pans and knock them about the kennel, water should be kept in a heavy crock. . . . There is no better breeding place for fleas than in the debris of a dirty bed."

Jo read that some kennels keep an individual log of each dog on which is noted any deviation from normal routine. She discovered that it would be necessary to compile a complete record of every transaction, and that the office should be as businesslike as the kennel should be shipshape.

By the time Dr. Webster pulled into the drive she wasn't nearly so certain as she had been that a seventeen-year-old girl could tackle the job and make a go of it. She even began to hope that perhaps the runs would be in such bad condition that the cost of repair would be prohibitive. Feeling younger and more incompetent than she had when she was a freshman in high school, Jo walked across the lawn to meet the vet.

"I've got just about five minutes," Uncle Doc said with more than his usual briskness. "Then I've got to chase up-country beyond Downingtown to look at a sick horse."

Jo found herself following his substantial back toward the kennels. "I've been thinking—" she started to say, but got no farther.

"Say, these aren't in bad shape!" the veterinarian exclaimed. He put his hand on a corner post supporting the six-foot-high wire of one row of pens, and attempted to shake it. "Welded fencing, best there is." He opened a gate and ducked through to the enclosure. "Let's take a look at the flooring in the houses. H'm. Fair. Could use some patching. The same goes for the roofs."

He walked up and down the path between the runs, then around to the rear of the houses, testing a post here and there, thumping a roof. His eyes narrowed as he tried to approximate the cost of repair.

"You know Tony Smith?" he asked Jo.

"The carpenter?"

"Yep. Tony could spend a day here and get you in shape. Time plus material would probably run you fifty dollars, no more. Ask him for an estimate, though, to be on the safe side."

"But, Uncle Doc—"

The veterinarian didn't seem to hear. "Tell you what I'll do—when's your mother coming home?"

"Not until sometime this evening."

Dr. Webster nodded. "You hop in my car and I'll drop you off and let you talk to my kennelman. Ben's a good sort. Little crude, but knows his business. You ask him all the questions you want, and he can answer 'em. Handled hundreds of dogs in his day, has Ben."

Jo found herself propelled into Uncle Doc's car almost against her will. She murmured something about having dinner to get and Ricky to supervise, but the vet paid no attention. "Won't take you more'n an hour," he insisted. "You'll learn a lot. And I'll have Ben run you back home."

Ten minutes later Jo found herself being introduced to a tall, thin man with a receding chin.

"Ben, you take Miss Josie over the place and give her an earful," Uncle Doc commanded. "She's got an idea she wants to run a summer boarding kennel, over at the old MacNeill place, and I'm aimin' to send her some business if she can work the thing out."

Ben looked a little nonplussed, but he was cooperative enough. "All you need to run a boarding kennel is common sense and a likin' for dogs," he told Jo. "And shade, plenty of shade. Dogs don't like to lie out in the broilin' sun."

"We have enough shade over at our place," Jo told

24

him meekly. She also mentioned her liking for dogs, but she wasn't sure what claim she had to the primary requirement of common sense. In Ben's conception, that probably covered a lot of ground.

He took her back to the kennels, where a dozen dogs greeted her with noisy enthusiasm, until Ben calmed them down. "We're not full-up yet," he explained. "Our peak season's between Fourth of July and Labor Day. Then we could use twice this much space."

This was the most encouraging information he could possibly have offered to Jo. Her enthusiasm began to return. July and August were the very months during which she wanted to take in boarders!

She asked Ben about details of running a kennel, and he explained how and where to buy canned meat and kibble in quantity, and how to calculate portions for dogs of different sizes. Jo found that since big dogs like Danes, mastiffs, and St. Bernards cost considerably more to feed than small animals, their board bills would be proportionately higher.

"Heck, it's got to be that way," Ben said. "A Dane eats two to three pounds of meat a day."

Jo was introduced by the kennelman to a setter who was so homesick he refused to eat at all, and to a hound who crouched in the corner of his pen and trembled. "These are both new boarders," Ben explained. "They'll come around in a few days."

Jo squatted before the hound's pen and tried to coax him to come to her. "What makes him so scared?"

"He's got a bad case of claustrophobia," Ben told her.

"Claustrophobia?"

25

"Yep. Never been penned up before. Dogs get sick from it, just like people. He'll get over it, but it may take a while."

Opening the gate, Ben snapped a leash on the dog's collar and took the hound in his arms, stroking his back and talking to him gently. Gradually the dog quieted, and even wagged his tail, but when the kennelman put him back in the enclosure he backed off and started to tremble again.

Most of the dogs, however, seemed happy and healthy to Jo. Reared in a house where, except at rare intervals, there had always been a dog around, she responded at once to the eloquence of the soft eyes looking at her through the wire.

Only the business end of running a summer boarding kennel alarmed her. She was positive she could handle the dogs—and love it! The idea of coping with many different canine personalities didn't sound like work. It sounded like fun.

But what would her mother think of the notion? Suppose she reacted, as Steve had, with instant disapproval?

3

JO RECKONED without the support of Uncle Doc. Originally dubious, he began to see a summer boarding kennel as a paying proposition, and stopped by after office hours that evening to inquire about Jo's father and give her idea a boost.

Ellen Redmond, exhausted by nervous strain and the long drive back from the rest home in the Poconos, was apathetic. She lay in a lounge chair and listened to Luke Webster as she might have listened to Ricky telling her an involved story about something that had happened at school. Her eyes, soft brown like Jo's, were turned toward her old friend, but her mind wasn't on what he was saying.

When Jo broke in with the plea that she be allowed to go ahead with her plans, she said, "Darling, you and Uncle Doc decide. If you don't think the dogs would bark too much at night—"

Afterward, out on the porch, Dr. Webster slipped his arm through Jo's and drew her toward him. "Do your mother good to get her mind off your dad," he whispered. "Can't tell, the dogs might help. At least they'll provide activity around the place, and the summer won't seem so long."

The summer was beginning to seem too short to Jo, as she followed her mother upstairs a few minutes later. With all she had to do to get ready for her boarders, the long June days would fly. But she didn't talk that night about the million and one details that would have to be settled tomorrow. She was very gentle and solicitous with her mother, helping unpack her overnight bag, drawing her a hot bath, turning down her bed.

When Jo finally said good night, she made her mother smile with her grandmotherly advice. "Now don't you worry, Mommy, Dad's going to be all right. He'll have the very best care. And you and Ricky and I can make out just fine. You'll see!"

If breakfast the next morning was a sample of how they could "make out just fine," the next couple of months would not be so peaceful as Jo had promised. To begin with, Ricky came clattering downstairs with his shirt on wrong side out, his hair uncombed, and an almost visible chip on his shoulder.

He didn't seem to notice that his mother's eyes were tired and worried, and that there were lines of strain around her mouth. It was a warm day, really warm, and he was filled with one increasing purpose. He wanted to go swimming, and he had to have twenty-four dollars for his season membership at the Dam.

"Everybody's been swimming all week," he announced as though it were the only important thing in the world. "Everybody but me!" He looked at both his

28

mother and Jo reproachfully.

"So what?" muttered Jo under her breath.

"So I've gotta have twenty-four bucks," Ricky said, impervious to family distress. "And I can't find my trunks. I've looked everywhere."

"Maybe the trash man got them," suggested Jo maliciously.

Ricky ignored her. "Mom, when can I have the money?"

"I'm not at all sure that you are going to be able to join Martin's Dam this summer."

Jo could tell that her mother was keeping her voice calm with an effort, but Ricky was unconscious of any such nuance. "Not join the Dam?" he squawked, pushing back his chair and leaving part of a fried egg forgotten on his plate. "You're kidding!"

Ellen Redmond turned and faced her son. "No, Ricky, I'm not."

"Well, what the heck?" Ricky was more puzzled than alarmed as yet. "All the kids belong. You know that, Mom. I always have other years. What goes?"

"There happens," broke in Jo tartly, "to be a slight question of money."

Mrs. Redmond, more understanding of a small boy's psychology than her daughter, tried to explain. "You see, Rick, Dad's expenses are going to be high. And while the bank will pay him something during the time he's away, there will be nothing like a full salary coming in. You're old enough to understand some of these things."

Ricky refused to be mollified by his mother's attempt to talk to him like an equal. He understood only one thing

—that his summer's fun was being threatened—and he was prepared to do battle for what he considered his rights.

One loophole occurred to him. Mom had said, "I'm not sure." She hadn't actually said, "You can't." He ate the rest of his cold egg in a couple of gulps and searched for a new line of attack.

From under her lashes, Jo watched her brother's face. Every thought that crossed his brain was pictured there, and Jo suddenly realized—because she could recall being nine years old herself—how desperate he must feel.

With a quick change of heart she put down her fork and leaned forward. "Tell you what, Ricky, I'll take you into business with me," she proposed. "You can earn the money to join the club, maybe. If you'll work."

"Work?" The mere word was shocking. "Who wants to work?"

Jo shrugged and returned to her breakfast, unamused. "Forget it. It was just an idea."

Ricky spread orange marmalade thickly on a piece of toast and munched it in silence while he watched his mother, who showed no sign of relenting. "What kind of work?" he asked finally.

Jo was succinct. "Cleaning the dog pens out back."

"Aw creeps, what for?"

"I'm going to take some dogs to board this summer, maybe." Jo added the "maybe" in a detached tone of voice because it had just occurred to her that she would have to find something to use for money herself.

Fifty dollars, more or less, for Tony Smith, paint for the houses, cedar shavings for bedding, meat and kibble. On seventy-five or eighty dollars—anticipating that the owners of some of her first boarders would be willing to pay in advance—she might just squeeze through.

"Dogs to board?" Ricky was saying as Jo considered her possible assets. "Here?"

His sister nodded. "I'm going to fix up the kennels for them." There were her graduation checks, twenty-eight dollars in all, and the thirty dollars left in her savings account, if Mother would let her draw it out.

"Hey!" she heard Ricky grumbling, interrupting her thoughts. "You can't use the corral. Me 'n Toby have to have a place for a pasture."

"Toby and I," corrected Mrs. Redmond, between sips of coffee.

"King of the Wind and Thunderhead," murmured Jo, "are going to have to roam the range this summer."

"Who says?"

"I say." Jo's voice was firm. "Now look, Ricky, do you want to make some money or don't you?" To punctuate her question she pulled the lever of the toaster down with a clack.

Ricky glanced at his mother, who looked detached from the conversation. Jo knew he was reckoning his chances of wheedling a swimming club membership by waiting for a more auspicious time.

"What will you pay me?" he mumbled finally.

Jo had the answer ready. "A dollar an hour, if you earn it."

"Only a dollar? Jim Patterson earns more than that cutting grass. Besides, it's below the minimum wage!"

"Jim's three years older than you. You're below the

minimum age," Jo reminded him. "Listen, brother, you'd better decide whether you intend to take it or leave it, because if you don't want the job, I'm going to call up Toby Apple and offer it to him."

That clinched the matter. If Toby was employed, Ricky would have no sidekick. He might as well assure his swimming club membership and get in on the deal himself.

Before he could change his mind, Jo hurried him back to the weed-grown runs and put him to work. For the first half hour, until he seemed to understand what was needed, she worked along with him. Then she left him to his own devices and went back to the house to telephone Tony Smith.

Tony was tied up for the day, but he allowed he could come over about sundown and look the situation over. Jo thanked him politely, then tackled her mother on the subject of her savings account.

Mrs. Redmond could see that if Jo took both her graduation money and her savings it would be less than enough to get her launched. She was as cooperative as possible, and was willing to lend Jo twenty dollars, but she warned her daughter that she mustn't get into this project over her head.

Relieved, and doubly enthusiastic now that the money question was presumably settled, Jo gave her mother a thankful hug and hurried off in the family car to buy paint for the kennels. Gray, she thought. With red for the long, sloping roofs. But when she priced paint she found she couldn't afford two gallons, and whitewash was so much cheaper that she decided to whitewash the side walls,

32

inside and out, and buy red barn paint for the roofs.

Coming out of the hardware store, laden with her purchases, she bumped into Ginny Clark.

"Goodness," Ginny trilled as she stood back and read the label on a can. "You look as if you're going into business."

"I am," said Jo. "Got ten minutes? I'll buy you a Coke and tell you about it."

She was feeling expansive this morning and full of vitality. Ginny needed no persuasion to cross the street to the drugstore, and together the two girls climbed onto the high stools along the soda fountain, which was practically deserted at this time of day.

Jo knew that Steve was on duty only during the afternoon and evening rush hours, so there was no danger that his presence behind the counter would hamper their talk. She poured out all her plans to Ginny, scarcely aware of her friend's astonishment.

"Don't you think it will be fun?" she ended breathlessly.

Ginny hedged. "It sounds like a big undertaking."

"It's going to be a lot of work," Jo admitted. "But if I make some money—"

"Won't you mind the—messiness?"

"I may." Jo was honest. "But that's a small part of the job. I'll love having all the dogs to feed and walk and play with."

"Who's going to have all whose dogs?" A voice behind her made Jo swing around on her stool.

"Oh, hello, Chuck!" A merry-eyed boy, almost stout enough to be called obese, stood smiling at her. "I've

33

been telling Ginny I'm going to run a summer boarding kennel. If I can get any customers! Free advertising gratefully acknowledged," she added as an afterthought.

Chuck rocked back on his heels. "Not a bad idea, not bad at all," he acknowledged. "You have those old runs back of your place, haven't you?" He put a hand on Ginny's shoulder. "Move over a seat and let me in between you beautiful babes. This I must explore."

Though Ginny was less than enthusiastic about Jo's plan, Chuck was sufficiently keen to make up for it. "Don't see why you shouldn't get rich, Josie. Best idea for a summer job I've heard of yet!"

Bolstered by such encouragement, Jo worked zealously all afternoon. Ricky, she found on arriving home, had slowed down to a snail's pace during her absence, but even this failed to dismay her. She told him the amount he could reasonably be expected to accomplish in an hour, and said if he fell short of the mark, she'd put his pay on a piecework basis. Then, closing her ears to his howls of protest, she started to scythe the tall grass in the abandoned exercise pen.

During the next couple of days Jo found that Ricky could be counted upon for two-hour stretches of effort, no more. She utilized him when she could, then let him go about his own concerns with good grace. After all, he was only nine.

With Tony Smith she had better luck. Tony came as he had promised, looked the situation over, and agreed to do the patch work that was necessary with some lumber from the Redmonds' cellar.

"How much will it be?" Jo asked timidly.

34

"Too much," replied Tony wryly. "It's always too much."

Jo's heart fell, but she managed a smile. "I'm a poor girl trying to work my way through college," she told him, then laughed at the fact that her remark was not far from the truth.

The carpenter scratched his head and made some penciled calculations on a grubby sheet of paper. "With the found lumber, let's say we make it forty dollars." He looked at her quizzically. "Can you stand that?"

Jo could have thrown her arms around his weather-beaten neck, but she said sedately, "That's within my budget."

Tony nodded. "Want I should start tomorrow?"

"That would be marvelous, if you could!"

"Everybody always wants me to start tomorrow," the carpenter said with a sigh. But Jo's bright eyes and ready smile were winning. "All right," he agreed suddenly. "For you I'll tell Mrs. Abercrombie the shoe shelves for her closet will have to wait."

Jo thanked him profusely, and was delighted when, the next morning, Tony proved as good as his word. She and Ricky had gathered and burned great piles of leaves, pine needles, and accumulated refuse from the pens. The wire was easy to get at, the places to be patched clearly discernible, but Jo asked Tony to take care of the wood repairs first so that she could start painting at the earliest possible moment. The Redmond place rang with the productive sound of hammering all day, and when Dr. Webster stopped by the next morning Jo was ready to begin whitewashing the pens.

"Hi, Uncle Doc!" she called from the back of the yard. "Come see."

The veterinarian sauntered toward the kennels, stopping to rough up Ricky on the way. "You're going to be shipshape in no time!" he approved, keeping an arm around the boy's shoulders. "Good thing too. Ben phoned this morning and said we've had a sudden rush of business. Our kennels are almost full, which is unusual for June."

Jo stood and looked toward her own dog runs. They still looked neglected and shabby, unoccupied and unpainted as they were. But she could visualize them a week hence, ready for the first of her paying guests.

"How do you think you're going to like Jo's summer boarders?" Uncle Doc was asking Ricky, as he tilted the boy's chin up with an affectionate hand.

"Jo's summer boarders." The phrase had a Louisa May Alcott ring to it that made Jo laugh. It reminded her of *Jo's Boys,* an old book tucked away in the attic with other forgotten volumes of a century past.

"I'm a partner in the business," Ricky was telling Uncle Doc proudly. "See those runs? I cleaned 'em out. See that hedge? I clipped it." His chest seemed to swell.

Dr. Webster winked at Jo over Ricky's head. "While Jo's just been standing around giving orders, I suppose?"

Jo nodded. "Why, sure!"

After the veterinarian had gone, however, she discovered that Ricky had disappeared, how she couldn't have told. But at some moment when her head was turned her partner had simply vanished. He didn't turn up until

36

noon, when hunger drove him to the kitchen. Then, after lunch, when Jo went back to her tedious job of white-washing, he disappeared again. She was annoyed but not especially surprised. She knew Ricky. The first enthusiasm had worn off. From now on it would be hard to corner him for even half an hour at a time.

Jo worked that evening until six thirty, because the light was good and because she was so anxious to see some results from her efforts. By the time she stopped, her eyes smarted and her back ached with weariness. The hand in which she had held the heavy whitewash brush trembled when she tried to hold a fork, and she trudged upstairs immediately after dinner.

"Take it easy, darling!" her mother urged her. "You always dive into things so."

It was true, and Jo knew it. All through high school she had always plunged headfirst into something that interested her. "Just like your father," her mother would say, shaking her head affectionately, yet with a certain concern. "You burn up so much energy, you two."

Promising to go more slowly the next day, Jo fell asleep, and didn't awaken until a quail, calling from the apple tree outside her bedroom window, finally penetrated her consciousness with his insistent whistle.

She worked all morning, but after lunch Mrs. Redmond insisted that she knock off. Ginny phoned to ask her to play some tennis—Jane Allen, Ruth Reynolds, and she needed a fourth for doubles—so Jo's mother dropped her off at the courts on her way to do an errand in town.

The June day was fresh and mild, perfect tennis

weather. The girls played two sets, then relinquished the court to some waiting boys, and sat down on a bench on the sidelines.

Jo felt relaxed and happier than she had been since her father's departure. "That really took out the kinks," she murmured to Ginny. "I've been practically living in a whitewash pail, and I needed a change of pace."

"What have you been whitewashing?" Ruth asked idly. "The cellar?"

Jo shook her head. "Dog pens. I'm going into the dog-boarding business. Haven't you heard?"

She told Jane and Ruth all about it, saying, "Of course it'll be a week or so before I'm ready to open. There's a lot to do yet. But when I'm ready I hope you'll spread the word."

Ruth looked a little disturbed. "Do you think people will want to trust their pets to a girl?" A girl without any experience, her tone implied.

"Dr. Webster is to be on call for any emergency," Jo explained.

Jane chopped at the turf between her feet with the wooden frame of her tennis racket. "Ugh," she murmured. "I can imagine playing nursemaid to one dog, but to a dozen? Golly, I'd rather scrub floors."

Ginny, always loyal in an emergency, leaped to her friend's defense. "But you don't love dogs the way Jo does."

Jane shrugged. "I guess not."

Jo could feel her shoulders stiffen and her smile become fixed. Had they begun to treat her with a slight condescension—or was she imagining things? Jo glanced at her wristwatch. "Well," she murmured, keeping her voice as normal as possible, "should we be breaking loose?"

Ginny dropped her off before the others, and Jo ran up the lane as the station wagon started on down the road. From the outside the Redmond house looked peaceful and empty, but Jo could see that the car was back in the garage. Humming a cheerful tune in an effort to dispel her resentment at Jane's attitude, Jo took the porch steps two at a time.

The screen door banged behind her. Tennis racket still in hand, she stopped abruptly at the living room door. Her mother was sitting in the wing chair and Ricky was poised on the very edge of the couch. Both turned toward Jo.

But Jo had eyes only for the third occupant of the room, a large, loose-skinned Great Dane puppy who was attached to a couch leg by a sturdy leash.

4

"WELL, WHAT—?" Jo started.

"I found him here with Ricky when I came home," said Mrs. Redmond, as though this explained a good deal. Her eyes were twinkling with amusement.

"I don't see why everybody acts so surprised," Ricky complained. He faced Jo with an injured expression. "You said you were going to run a boarding kennel, didn't you? So we've got a boarder."

As though he understood, the Great Dane got to his feet with youthful awkwardness and wagged his tail.

"Where did he come from?" Jo crossed the room and stroked the pup's ear, cradling his big head in her hand.

"Some woman brought him."

Jo looked at Ricky sternly. "Who?"

"Some woman named Mrs.—oh, gee, what did she say?" Ricky frowned, trying to remember. "Anyway, she said Dr. Webster had told her about us," he added happily.

"Didn't you tell her we weren't open for business yet?"

"I thought we were. Any time we got some dogs."

40

"Ricky Redmond, have you taken a good look at those kennels? Half whitewashed, wire still to be repaired, no bedding—"

"He could sleep with me."

"He could not," interjected Mrs. Redmond with conviction.

Jo sat down beside her mother. "Tell me the story from the beginning, Ricky. Did this woman phone before she brought him over—and by the way, what's his name?"

"Roger," said Ricky, answering the last question first.

The Dane lifted his pointed ears, and at the same moment the telephone rang.

"She said she'd call back later," Ricky informed Jo hastily. "Maybe that's her now."

"Miss Redmond?" came a rather anxious voice at the other end of the wire in answer to Jo's hello.

"Yes?"

"Oh, I'm so glad! This is Mrs. Peter McCallum, on Upper Gulph Road. You have my dog."

"The Dane puppy? But—" Jo started.

"I was sorry not to see you personally," the voice raced on. "But, frankly, I've been in the most frightful rush. My husband and I are leaving for California tonight, quite unexpectedly. And we simply couldn't find anyone who could take Roger. Then Dr. Webster suggested you, and it was such a rude thing to do, just drop him off, but your little brother assured me—"

Mrs. McCallum paused, and Jo made a quick decision. "Actually, we're not open for business yet, but we'll be glad to keep him. However, I haven't figured out what the rate for a Great Dane should be."

"Oh, anything will be all right, anything that you and Dr. Webster feel is fair. It's such a relief—you just don't know!—to be able to go off and be sure he's in good hands."

"I hope!" breathed Jo under her breath. Aloud, trying to be businesslike, she said, "May I have your exact address, and will there be any way of getting in touch with you in California?"

For a minute or two she scribbled rapidly on the telephone pad, spelling back some of the words. Then she said, "Yes, we'll be sure that he gets enough exercise. Yes, indeed. And we'll count on keeping him until the twenty-eighth. Thank you very much. Good-by."

When Jo walked back into the living room she was smiling. "Five weeks," she murmured to her mother with lifted eyebrows. "I take it all back, Ricky. You're a bright boy. Five weeks of Roger will be quite a tidy little sum."

"What's my commission?"

"Commission?"

"Sure," Ricky said, "I got him for you, didn't I?"

"You just happened to be home when he arrived," Jo told him firmly. "You're still working for a dollar an hour, brother dear."

Ricky stood up, dug his hands into the pockets of his jeans, and stamped toward the door. "Tightwad!" he muttered as he passed Jo.

"Eric!" Mrs. Redmond only used her son's full name when she was scolding.

"Well, she is!" Ricky cried, undaunted. "And just because you're so mean, I won't let Roger sleep in my room after all!"

Roger, as a matter of fact, spent the first two nights of his residence with the Redmonds curled up on a rag rug at the foot of Jo's bed. She could hear him snoring peacefully when she awakened in the morning. If she shifted position he would hear her, sit up and stretch, then pad softly around the bed to see whether her eyes were open and it was time to greet the day.

"You're a sweet baby," Jo told the big pup the second morning. "I'll bet Mrs. McCallum spoils you rotten. Does she, Roger?" She put out a hand and let him nuzzle her palm.

It was astonishing, she reflected, as she lay looking out the window, how adaptable a puppy could be. No grown dog would so immediately have accepted the change in domicile, but Roger already seemed at home.

Jo scratched the Dane's head behind an ear and the dog took a step forward and began to lick her neck. His tongue tickled, so Jo gathered his head in her arms, and he stood quiet and wagged his tail. "I wonder if you'd stay around if you were loose?" she asked him, and because her voice was soft and pleasant, Roger wagged his tail even harder. "Does that mean yes?"

"It would be fun to let you run, but I guess I'd better not," Jo said with a sigh, sitting up in bed. "Uncle Doc says it's foolish to take chances. Dogs do the darnedest things."

She stretched and yawned, pulling her coppery hair from her neck and gathering it on top of her head. From the bed she could see herself in her dressing table mirror, and the reflection didn't please her. There were dark half

43

circles under her eyes, and one forearm was streaked with red paint.

There was paint under her fingernails, too, and she had scratched the back of her right hand on a splintered board. Mercurochrome painted the angry red welt. Wrinkling her nose with distaste, Jo pushed at the puffy skin on either side of the cut. She didn't want to take any chances with infection.

From the bathroom across the hall came sounds of Ricky brushing his teeth. Mrs. Redmond always said that the amount of noise he made was out of all proportion to the results obtained.

Jo's father put it differently. "Ricky's ablutions are always performed with an eye to stage business," he contended. "If the family can hear the water running, he considers himself washed."

Sneakers padded downstairs, a screen door slammed, and Jo swung her long legs to the floor. The bathroom would now be empty.

As she crossed the hall in her bare feet she thought about the number of times her mother and dad had discussed putting in a second bath. But there had been Jo's appendectomy, Ricky's teeth to straighten, now her dad's illness. Oh, well! The old-fashioned fixtures in the present bathroom were familiar and comfortable, and the sun streaming through the open window speckled the walls with light.

Jo leaned her elbows on the sill, pressed her forehead against the screen, and looked over the side yard toward the rear of the house. The back hedge was entirely clipped now, and beyond it she could glimpse the bright-

44

red roofs of the kennels. The sight made the smudge of paint on her arm seem worthwhile, yet she walked to the washbasin and scrubbed at the smear vigorously. "One day more," she murmured to herself.

However, one day more for the painting job lengthened to three when a sudden influx of business presented Jo with a Scottie, a dachshund, and a cocker spaniel. Now, including Roger, there were four dogs to house, water, feed, and exercise.

Fortunately, Tony Smith showed up to do the last of the fence-patching, and Jo had no fear that the dogs would be insecure. Roger, placed in a pen adjoining the others, looked down upon his smaller neighbors with equanimity, yet it took every bit of willpower Jo possessed to leave him in the kennel overnight, when she knew he would much rather have returned to the rug at the foot of her bed.

But this was a business she was running, and she was determined to be businesslike about it. At a stationery store Jo bought an account book, and in it she listed the names of the owners and the dates of arrival of her four dogs.

Departure Date, she wrote in another column. And in still another, Rate Per Day. Her mother leaned over her shoulder and made a suggestion or two. "Though I'm no bookkeeper," she amended. "You really should have your father here."

Only through the tenderness that crept into her voice whenever she mentioned her husband did Ellen Redmond betray how much she missed him. Jo, sensitive to her mother's mood, looked up. "I could write and tell him what I'm doing," she suggested. "Maybe Dad would have some ideas." Then she hesitated. "Or do you think it would tire him?"

"I think he'd love it. He's probably bored to distraction by now."

So that night Jo wrote to her father.

"I'm in business!" she told him. "But I need some advice, and you're elected. Here's the setup. The Redmond Boarding Kennels officially opened today."

In sprawling, uphill handwriting Jo described the launching of her summer venture, giving Uncle Doc all the credit she knew he deserved. "Of course he says, 'It will be the end of a beautiful friendship if your father finds out I've had a hand in this.' But I know better. If you could see the kennels, with their new red roofs!

"And the dogs! Daddy, you'd love the dogs. We have a six-month-old Great Dane puppy with the most appealing eyes and beautiful manners. We have a Scottie, named Mac of course, and a merry little dachshund who wiggles like crazy whenever Ricky appears. And later this afternoon a lady who was the image of Lucille Ball brought in the fattest cocker spaniel you ever saw. Called Bitsy, natch.

"I've been thinking a card system might be a good idea, with the name of the dog, and the owner, and some room for 'pertinent facts.'

" 'Pertinent facts' are what Mother calls the things that owners generally tell you. Things like, 'Bitsy has slept on this pillow since she was three months old, so I just brought it along.' It's easy, with only four dogs, to remember names and whose leash is whose and special diet

46

requirements, but if this business gets really rolling, I'll need more than a memory, so what do you suggest?''

Jo kept on writing, filling page after page of paper, for the first time in her life having so much to talk about that she couldn't seem to stop.

Her mother had sent Ricky to bed long since, and about ten thirty she went upstairs herself, leaving Jo sitting with her legs curled around the rungs of the desk chair, her pen still flying.

"Coming soon, dear?" Mrs. Redmond called from her bedroom door.

"In a minute."

But the minute stretched to ten, then twenty. Finally Jo gathered her letter together, folded the sheets of paper, and tucked them, fat and bulging, into an envelope. "There."

She leaned the envelope against the desk lamp and trudged upstairs with a sense of satisfaction. "Dad'll know more about the dog business than I know myself!" she told her mother, who was reading in bed.

Mrs. Redmond put out a hand, and Jo went across the room and took it in both her own.

"You look tired, Josie."

"I'm not, really."

"Don't work too hard. Don't spoil your summer. You really should have gone swimming when Ginny phoned today."

"I'm going tomorrow," Jo promised.

She ran a strand of hair through her fingers, and wrinkled her nose. "It's in my way, these days. I think I'll cut it short, like yours. Then we'll get Ricky to take a snapshot

47

of us to send to Dad. He'll think we look like sisters."

Jo's voice was lighthearted, but she avoided meeting her mother's eyes because she didn't want her to guess that behind her cheerfulness the disappointment over college was still intense.

A few minutes later she turned to go into her own room. "Aren't the doggies being good?" she asked over her shoulder. "Not a bark out of them."

But she spoke too soon. For the next two hours the kennel's occupants slumbered as peacefully as the Redmond household. Then, out of a deep sleep, Jo sat bolt upright.

High and eerie on the night air rose a dog's howl. It was a strange sound, like a thin scream, gradually ascending to higher notes and greater volume. Before it reached a peak it was accompanied by a gruff, adolescent bark immediately recognizable as Roger's, and by the quick, sharp yaps of a Scottie and a dachshund.

Jo felt for her scuffs and reached for a robe blindly. What a din, considering there were only four dogs penned out back!

In the hall she nearly crashed, head on, into Ricky, who was fumbling for the electric light switch. "Oops!"

The child faced her in the sudden glare, looking younger than his age in his faded pajamas. "D'you s'pose a little old fox is out there?" he asked hopefully.

"Fox? What are you talking about?" Jo scoffed, but her heart was pounding as she raced downstairs. Something certainly must be wrong.

"There *are* foxes around here! Toby saw one." Ricky came trotting along at his sister's heels, apparently anxious to be in on any drama the night might provide.

Jo hurried through the dark house, switching on the kitchen light and fumbling with the lock on the back door. For the first time she felt the overwhelming sense of responsibility that was to attack her again and again during the summer. These dogs had been left in her charge. They were hers to guard and to protect. What if something happened to even one of them? How could she ever face the owner?

The boards of the back porch were silvered and the moon made a white patch on the lawn. With every passing moment the barking of the dogs was becoming more frenzied. Jo kicked off her slippers on the steps, and started in her bare feet across the dew-wet grass, Ricky still following.

Suddenly she stopped and sniffed, and a wave of relief flooded through her.

"Skunk!"

"Skunk?" Ricky echoed, in a voice of complete disgust. "Aw, when it could've been a fox!"

"You go back to bed," Jo said. "I'll take care of the dogs." Already she was calling them by name. "Roger! Mac! Bitsy! Quiet now. Good dogs. Quiet."

5

THE SUN, beaming down on the raft at Martin's Dam, had a seashore bite to it, but the air remained cool. The trees at the pool's edge were June-green, the sky as blue as a Pennsylvania sky can be. Jo stood looking out over the water as she pulled on her swimming cap. She felt as if she had been away for a long time and had just come home.

This was summer as it should be—as it had always been. The gang lolling on the raft, the long, lazy afternoons, the talk and fooling around. All this Jo had missed, without realizing that she was missing it, so absorbed had she been in getting her dog business launched.

Chuck sat up on the raft and peered over the water, saw Jo and waved. "Come on out!"

Ginny, beside him, raised herself to her elbows and watched Jo dive.

Coming up, Jo shouted, "It's cold!"

"It's always cold, but it feels good after you get wet."

The routine remarks, pleasant and uncomplicated, were called back and forth.

50

"I signed in under your name, Ginny, and paid my guest fee. That all right?"

"You know it is, Jo. Sorry you couldn't come yesterday, but today's even better." Ginny turned over to lie flat on her back.

Bill Hamilton pulled himself out of the water on the other side of the raft just as Jo's head appeared above the steps.

"Hi, Jo."

"Hi, Bill."

No fuss, no necessity for small talk. The same old crowd.

Then a girl with pale-blond hair who had been lying beside Ginny pushed herself to her knees and took a good look at Jo. Ginny waved a hand in the girl's direction. "Gail Chartriss, Jo Redmond. Gail's a new neighbor of ours, Jo. Her family bought the Marshall place, you know."

Jo had a feeling she should have known, but memory eluded her. She nodded at Gail, smiled and said, "Hello," but she was sorry—and was half-ashamed of being sorry —that a newcomer was present.

"Hi, there." Something in the way the blond girl looked at her disturbed Jo. Had they been talking about her just now? she wondered.

Annoyed at herself for feeling ill at ease, Jo made conversation. "That's a beautiful house, the Marshalls'. I've never been inside, but I should think you'd love living there."

Gail raised her eyebrows, which had been cleverly penciled. "It's going to need redecorating," she said.

51

Ginny shaded her eyes from the sun and yawned. "Take off your cap and stay a while, Jo."

Jo unsnapped the chin strap and pulled the cap off with a quick gesture. Ginny, watching her, sat up and squealed. "You've cut your hair!"

Jo nodded. "It was in my way."

Cocking her head thoughtfully to one side, Ginny considered. "I like it. Yes, I really do. It curls more, short. Don't you like it, Chuck?"

Chuck's plump stomach rippled with laughter. "Girls. How should I know? Sure. Sure, it looks swell."

"That's what I love about Chuck," Jo said sardonically. "So sincere."

She wasn't certain, herself, whether she liked what she had done to her hair. It made her feel different, almost boyish. The soft halo around her head thinned her cheekbones and made her features seem more distinct. She wondered what Steve would think of it when he saw her. Except to wave to, in passing, she hadn't seen him since the evening of their argument.

Gail moved over to sit beside Bill and swing her legs over the edge of the raft. "Are you going to Princeton too?" Jo heard her ask.

"Nope. I'm for Cornell along with Steve Chance, if he can raise the dough." Bill was always blunt.

Ginny turned her head. "Steve always wanted to be a doctor when he was a little kid. Does he still?"

Bill shrugged. "It takes a lot of time and money to study medicine."

"Who is Steve Chance?" asked Gail.

"One of the bright boys in our class at school," Ginny

52

told her. "That sounds stuffy, but I don't mean it to. Steve's quite a guy. Captain of the football team in addition to having a few brains."

Chuck's eyes were twinkling. "I never knew Steve was interested in medicine."

"Well, maybe he's given up the idea."

"Or maybe he's decided to go into an allied business," suggested Chuck.

"What's that?" Jo asked.

"Pharmacy."

"Just because he's working in a drugstore! Chuck, you're a—"

"I know. I'm a comedian!" Chuck yawned contentedly. "Swell day, isn't it? Let's stop talking about Steve and discuss somebody interesting."

"Like you?" Jo asked with a grin.

"No, like you," Chuck said in quick retaliation. "How's the dog business, Jo?"

"Thriving, thanks. But this is my day off." She welcomed a way to change the subject. "Look! Isn't that Ruth Reynolds? What is she holding in her hand?"

A girl was swimming from shore holding one arm out of the water. She came toward the raft slowly, using an old-fashioned sidestroke, and a few yards away stopped and began to tread water. "Here!" she called. "Catch!"

It was Bill who caught the jumbo-size chocolate bar she had been carrying. "Now don't say I never give the party," Ruth told them all as she reached out to grasp the ladder. "Divide it before it melts."

Everybody laughed. "Just like a St. Bernard to the rescue!" commented Chuck.

Apparently Ruth had met Gail Chartriss, because she greeted her with the same casual "Hi!" she used for the rest of the crowd. Dripping and breathless, she sank down, cross-legged, in the one unoccupied spot on the raft, and announced, "I just beat Jane three straight sets at tennis, and for me that's good!"

"What was Jane doing," Chuck asked, still playing the funny boy, "holding the racket in her left hand?"

Ruth made a playful pass at him. "I'm improving, and if you don't believe it, I'll take you on."

"Tomorrow morning?"

"Tomorrow at ten thirty." They chatted together, arranging the date.

Gail was talking to Ginny, and Bill was doling out chunks of chocolate. Jane appeared from the direction of the parking lot, walked around to the diving board, and cut the water with a jackknife. Jo watched her swim toward them. The most athletic of the girls, she had a fast and easy crawl.

At the raft Jane scorned the steps and stretched out a hand toward Jo. Bracing herself, Jo pulled her aboard so that she turned and sat on the edge of the float.

"Thanks. Goodness, Jo, your hands are as hard as a boy's."

Jo could feel herself flushing as Gail glanced at her hands. "Calluses," she remarked. "I've been doing some rough work lately."

"Work? That's a four-letter word." Perhaps Gail only intended to be amusing, but Jo's discomfiture increased.

"Listen to the daughter-of-the-idle-rich," remarked Bill

above the laughter. "It's nice to have you with us, Gail. You lend a certain tone."

Gail took the teasing more gracefully than Jo. "I'm a Persian kitten at heart," she retorted. "Why not admit it?"

Out of the blue Jane asked, "Is that your yellow Triumph in the parking lot, Gail?"

Gail nodded. "Daddy gave it to me for a birthday present."

"It sounds easy if you say it quick," muttered Chuck in an undertone to Jo, who smiled at him absently because her attention was centered on Gail.

"I'm going to go get a drink of water," she found herself saying, because she wanted to get away. Gail's presence was somehow spoiling the afternoon. Or was she uncomfortable because she felt curiously detached from the interests and activities of the crowd?

Swimming lazily toward shore, Jo scolded herself. Just because she was working there was no reason why the others shouldn't play. She hated spoilsports, always had. And she decided to make a special effort to be pleasant to Gail. If Ginny liked her, she must be a nice girl.

Jo went up to the clubhouse water bubbler, then stopped to talk to one of the lifeguards before she swam back to the raft. Crowded now, the float was riding low in the water. "Worse than a Philadelphia bus during the five o'clock rush," Chuck commented as she climbed back aboard. "Move to the back there! Make room for the lady!" He cleared a space for her.

Everybody was talking about taking a picnic lunch to a spot along the Brandywine, where Ruth's family had a rough weekend camp. "Two cars would do it," Jane said. "Could you take your station wagon, Ginny?"

"Probably, if I ask in advance."

"My car will only hold four," drawled Gail.

Ruth began to count noses. "You can go, can't you, Jo?"

"When?"

"Day after tomorrow."

Jo considered for a second. "I think you'd better count me out. There are six dogs in the kennels now. A boxer and another cocker came in this morning. I'm just getting this thing started, and a whole day—" Jo started to explain.

Gail overheard. "What thing? What are you doing, anyway? Are you digging for oil?"

Her questions fell in one of those pools of silence that occasionally drown conversation, and her final comment brought a laugh. Several heads turned toward Jo. "I'm running a summer boarding kennel," she said, her eyes meeting Gail's.

"Isn't Jo brave?" murmured Ginny.

"I think she's smart as all heck," said Chuck unexpectedly. "I wish I could dream up an idea as good."

"Don't the dogs howl at night?" Gail asked after a while.

"Not often." Jo told the group about the skunk, playing up Ricky's disappointment that it hadn't been a fox.

"Next time you ought to provide him with a deer," suggested Bill.

"Deer? Around here?" Gail turned incredulous violet eyes to meet his.

56

"Sure, I've seen deer in the woods back of Jo's place. That's country, back in there—not suburbs like this." He spread his arm inclusively, indicating the half-hidden houses in the hills surrounding the Dam.

The last thing from Bill's mind, Jo knew, was to belittle the location of the Redmonds' house, but he was classifying Jo as a country girl rather than a suburbanite.

Hiding her mouth with the back of her hand, Gail yawned daintily. "I think you're teasing," she told him. Then she turned her attention once more to Jo. "Have you had any experience in running a kennel?"

"Not really," Jo told her, trying to believe that the new girl didn't intend to be patronizing. "But I'm learning fast. And one of my father's best friends is Dr. Webster. He's on call for advice or help if I get stuck."

"Well, in that case, with the backing of a vet, I suppose it would be perfectly all right," Gail was saying.

"What would be all right?" Ginny wanted to know.

Gail waited until she again had the attention of the boys. "I was just thinking," she said, "that I might be able to send you some business." She looked up at Jo from under her lashes, but her eyes were cold.

Jo waited.

"We're going to Maine for the month of July, and I'm sure Mummy and Daddy will be willing to send you Trinket. She's our French poodle, and she's definitely a problem child. You know these imported purebred dogs."

Jo supposed she should say thank you politely, though she felt that she had never been treated with such condescension.

57

"Perhaps it would be wiser to put her in an established kennel," Jo said deliberately. She would have enjoyed quoting Uncle Doc's comment that a dog's personality usually reflects that of the owner, but she restrained herself. Pulling on her cap and getting to her feet, she added, "I've had enough sun. Anybody want to swim?"

6

"I'VE HAD ENOUGH, too, and I don't mean sun." Chuck's head broke the water four yards from the raft, and he turned on his back to float beside Jo.

"Sh!" Jo cautioned.

"I don't care. That girl's a bad actor."

"The rest of the crowd don't think so."

"You do," stated Chuck flatly. "Or you should."

"Oh, I rather enjoy being torn limb from limb," Jo fibbed ruefully. "Come on. I'll race you to the dock."

When they arrived, breathless, in what Chuck described as a photo finish, Jo decided she'd better be getting home. "I have six extra mouths to feed, and are they hungry!"

"I've got the Jeep. Can't I drive you and look over the bairns?"

"Of course you may." Jo was beginning to be sorry for all the occasions on which she had dismissed Chuck simply as a funny fat boy. He was a better friend than she had given him credit for. In the bathhouse she changed quickly to her clothes, met Chuck at the entrance of the parking area, and walked across the macadam at his side, wishing he were a little taller or that she were not quite so tall.

He opened the door for her and bowed gallantly. Jo stepped in and Chuck rounded the Jeep, squeezed under the wheel, and started the rackety motor. "Neat but not gaudy," he commented, "unlike that yellow job."

Jo turned to get a better look at Gail's smart car. She whistled softly. "Bet you'd trade!"

"Cars, not girls."

"Thank you, sir." Now if Steve had made that remark, Jo realized, she would have blushed like a twelve-year-old. But with Chuck, who was as comfortable as an old shoe, she could pass it off with a smile.

As the Jeep rattled out of the gate of the swimming club Jo could see through a break in the forsythia hedge that the crowd on the raft was thinning. Apparently most of the others had decided to go along home. She sat with her hands clasped in her lap, frowning a little because she was emotionally upset, although she wouldn't have admitted it for the world. And it wasn't entirely because of Gail. For the first time since she could remember she had felt a certain defection in Ginny. Ginny and she had always been so close. It was impossible that a week or two could pull them apart like this.

Yet this afternoon it had seemed to Jo that Ginny was merely an acquaintance. They shared a surface understanding, nothing more. It confused and disturbed her.

"Wake up, dog woman, we're home!" Chuck stopped the Jeep with a jerk in front of the Redmonds' garage.

Jo looked at him sharply. "Have you been talking to Steve?"

"Not seriously. Why?"

"He calls me Mrs. Truck."

"That's because he loves you. Like me."

Jo shook her head but had to laugh. Chuck was incorrigible. "Come along to the kennels and see the babes or, as Gail would probably call it, the menagerie."

"Leave us not be bitter," teased Chuck as he rolled amiably along in her wake. "Boy, you have spruced this place up!"

"First you must meet Roger, our star boarder." Jo introduced the Great Dane puppy, then the rest of the dogs. They waggled a welcome to Chuck, all except a red cocker who had been brought in that morning. He crouched in the corner of his pen, tongue lolling, eyes half closed. When Jo called him by name, he started toward the gate uncertainly.

"What's the matter, fellow?" Jo opened the wire door and crouched in the entryway. The cocker stood and looked at her, head hanging.

"Are you homesick, Sherry?"

Chuck said, "He looks ill."

"He doesn't seem to feel up to snuff, does he?" Jo's voice was troubled. "He just came in this morning. The people who own him have gone to the Poconos for two weeks."

Chuck bent over and stroked the cocker's soft head. "What's the matter with his eye?"

"His eye?" Jo knelt and took Sherry's muzzle in her

hand. His right eye was covered with a milky film, and as she ran her hand along the dog's back to bring him toward her for a closer inspection he suddenly yelped in pain.

She lifted her hand quickly, and found that it was red and sticky with blood. "Chuck, he's been hurt—badly!—but how?"

"He must have been flinging himself against the wire." Chuck pulled some tufts of red fur from the side of the pen, then crouched down and whistled. "Hey, look, Jo! There's a jagged tear here the size of my fist."

"Tony must have missed that one," Jo muttered, but her thoughts were on the dog—her responsibility, her charge. She regarded him with dismay. "I'd better call Uncle Doc."

Chuck agreed with her. "I'll hang around for a while in case he wants you to bring him over to the office," he proposed. "Might as well use the Jeep as get your car out."

Jo appreciated the moral support. She left Chuck out at the kennels, and went back toward the house at a trot, remembering that the cocker had seemed nervous on arrival, but she hadn't dreamed he would become violent. If only she had resisted the urge to go swimming and stayed on the job!

Inside, the house was dim and quiet.

"Mother!" No answering voice called back. There was a note on the kitchen table, however, scrawled hastily on a brown paper bag. "Elaine stopped by to ask me to help decide on some drapery fabric. Left Ricky in charge. Back shortly. Mother."

"Ricky in charge," snorted Jo as she walked through the house to the phone. So far as she had been able to tell, he was nowhere around.

Dr. Webster's line was busy. She waited, drumming impatiently on the telephone table. There was so much to be done in the late afternoon—the dogs to exercise and feed, water pans to be refilled, all sorts of minor chores.

Jo dialed again. Still busy.

It occurred to her that it would be a good idea to move the ailing cocker away from the other dogs, into the house. She ran back to the kennels, where Chuck was sitting on the ground with Sherry's head in his lap.

"Get the vet?"

"Not yet. The line's busy."

"Let's just buzz on over and take the chance he'll be home."

"That's a good idea," Jo agreed. She gathered the cocker's soft body into her arms, and followed Chuck to his Jeep. "I wish Ricky or Mother would show up. It's not right to leave the dogs alone with nobody on the place at all."

"Who said there's nobody on the place?"

A voice from the branches of the black walnut tree which shaded a corner of the garage made Jo stop and look up.

"Ricky! Well, you might at least have told me you were there."

"Why?"

"Try to answer that one, Josie," muttered Chuck under his breath.

"So I wouldn't be worried," replied Jo promptly, feeling she could have done better if she had had a minute to think.

Ricky peered down through the leaves. "Look," he said with a world-weary sigh, "Mom told me I was to stick around. I'm stickin'. She didn't say I was to keep you from worrying. So!"

On the way to the veterinarian's office, the cocker lay in Jo's lap and trembled. "When dogs are hurt or get sick," she remembered Uncle Doc saying, "they don't know what's gone wrong. People keep thinking, Tomorrow I'll be better, but not dogs. All a dog knows is that he feels terrible at the moment. He can't look forward, the way a person can, to getting well."

The glass-enclosed porch that stretched across the front of the Websters' house, serving as a waiting room for four-legged patients, was completely deserted at this time of the afternoon. Dr. Webster's office hours were from six to eight in the evening. Jo had only the busy signal on which to pin her hopes that she would find him at home.

Chuck pushed the bell to the consulting room, and Jo breathed a sigh of relief when Uncle Doc himself opened the door. He nodded to Chuck, then crossed the porch to where Jo was standing with Sherry in her arms.

"Hello, honey. Something wrong?"

His voice was comfortingly matter-of-fact, his manner relaxed and normal.

"This cocker has hurt himself."

Dr. Webster put his hand under the dog's chin and

looked briefly at the filmy right eye. Sherry shrank back against Jo and shivered nervously.

"Bring him in. We'll see what's wrong."

Jo glanced toward Chuck, but the boy said, "You go ahead. I'll wait here."

Tenderly, Jo put the cocker down on the metal-topped examining table. Dr. Webster turned the dog toward him, a hand under his chin. Sherry twitched away, but the veterinarian held his head and peered at the eye through an ophthalmoscope. Then he looked at Jo and whistled softly.

"Ulcerated," he said, then saw the cocker's bloody back. "What's he been doing, to rip himself apart like this?"

Jo gulped. "He must have become frantic at being in a strange place, and there was a tear in the wire of his pen."

"Tony forgot to fix it, I suppose, and you forgot to check it."

Jo nodded miserably.

"With a corneal ulceration and a pretty deep wound this pup's going to need some careful nursing. You'd better get in touch with the owner, Jo. Now then, hold his head. I'll clean him up a bit."

"The Keenes have gone to the mountains for two weeks," Jo told the doctor as he clipped the hair away from the edges of the torn skin. "They're way up on a lake beyond Canadensis. Ten miles from the village and no phone. I'll have to write."

Dr. Webster sighed. "Then I guess you're elected. It's

rough, because he'll have to have eye drops every three hours, and the dressing on his back will have to be changed once a day."

"But wouldn't it be better if you kept the dog here?" Jo asked with a rush. "I mean, if he's in as bad shape as you say, wouldn't it be better—"

The veterinarian was busy at his medicine cabinet with his back to Jo and the examining table. "Every three hours, day and night," he explained over his shoulder. "I go out on calls for hours at a time. I'm not around here the way you're around your house, Josie. I'm always on the run."

Jo nodded. "I see."

"We can give him his first eye drops now and I'll show you how to swab out the wound," Dr. Webster said. "You won't have a bit of trouble once you learn the technique. I've taught lots of clients to doctor their own dogs in cases like this."

But Jo felt as sick as Sherry looked. "I don't know," she began, then stopped and bit her lip. "I'll do my best."

"Atta girl!" Uncle Doc said as Jo watched his quick, capable fingers, which made everything look so easy.

"Think you've got the idea?"

"I guess so."

"You'll be all right," Dr. Webster promised cheerfully. "Remember in changing the dressing that everything must be sterile," he said as he handed her a package containing supplies. "I'll order the eye drops for you from the drugstore."

"How do I keep him from biting his back or scratching his eye?" Jo asked anxiously.

"That's easy. Make him a cardboard collar—a big, stiff one, sort of like an Elizabethan ruff—and fasten it securely around his neck. And I'd keep him in the house if I were you. There you can keep an eye on him. I've given you an envelope of prednisolone tablets. Give him one tablet morning and evening, to calm him down."

Jo thanked the doctor and went out to join Chuck in the waiting room. She told him, without going into detail, what was wrong, and he drove her home quickly.

"Anything else I can do? Like feed the dogs?"

"You're awfully nice, Chuck, but I can manage now." Jo hoped she sounded more confident than she felt.

"So long, then. I'll stop by in a day or two and see how you're getting on. But don't expect me to help with anything gory. I turn green at the sight of blood."

Jo nodded, understanding. She remembered a time, at school, when she had been working beside Chuck in the zoology lab. His knife had slipped as he was dissecting a frog and she remembered the way he had suddenly blanched, sinking down on the nearest stool. Some people were like that. They just couldn't help it.

As Jo carried Sherry into the house she decided that it was fortunate she wasn't as squeamish as Chuck. It was only her fear that she would lack dexterity and would hurt the little dog unnecessarily that troubled her.

She made a bed in an old packing box, and got her mother's permission to house the patient in the kitchen. The cocker seemed content to stay in his new quarters, and lay with his lower jaw propped on the edge of the box, his eyes closed, breathing heavily.

Nevertheless, Jo couldn't count on Sherry remaining

quiet. She found a big cardboard box and drew two concentric circles on the lid, making the smaller one the approximate diameter of the cocker's neck. Then she made a slit on one side and fitted it on the recumbent dog, who seemed to have lost the will to object to anything.

As her mother started preparations for dinner Jo scurried in and out, feeding the other five dogs and enlisting Ricky to help exercise them. When she finally came to the dinner table herself, she couldn't seem to eat much supper. She kept glancing at Sherry and wondering if his eyesight would be permanently damaged.

It was seven thirty before the dishes were finished. "Uncle Doc said he'd order the eye drops from Brett's, but I guess it was too late to catch the delivery. I'd better take the car and go over to town," Jo said.

"I'll run in for them if you like." Mrs. Redmond, recognizing her daughter's concern, was anxious to be helpful. "Wouldn't you rather stay with the dog?"

As the car pulled out of the drive Jo was relieved that she would have some time alone to pull herself together. Ricky was in the living room looking at television, and before her mother came back she would have to get a firm hold on her nerves. A boarding kennel owner has to expect accidents, even disasters, and meet problems unemotionally. A proper, mature, kennel manager wouldn't be sitting on the floor in front of Sherry's box, stroking his silky head and murmuring disconnected words of sympathy, "Poor baby . . . little fellow . . . strange house . . . wish I could help."

The sharp clack of the front door knocker cut into her

monologue, and Jo reluctantly scrambled to her feet and went to answer it.

"Oh, hello."

Steve Chance stood in the doorway, a small white package in his hand.

"Hi! You don't sound exactly cordial."

"I'm sorry," Jo apologized halfheartedly.

He held out the package. "Don't know what this is, but I noticed your name on it, so I said I'd drop it off on my way home."

"It's a special kind of eye drops. Mother just left for the drugstore. But it was thoughtful of you. Thanks, anyway."

"Who's sick? Ricky?"

Jo shook her head. "One of the dogs." It was the first direct admission she had made to Steve that her boarding kennel was an established fact.

"Oh? What's wrong?"

"Dr. Webster calls it a corneal ulceration." Jo's troubled brown eyes met Steve's gray ones. "The dog's a cocker. He cut his eye on a jagged piece of wire and tore his back badly—but it's the eye Uncle Doc seems most worried about. He could lose the sight—" What was inducing her to tell Steve all this? He wouldn't be interested.

But, surprisingly, he looked concerned. "Look here, Jo, if I could help—"

For a second Jo hesitated, remembering that Steve had wanted to be a doctor, that he had skillful hands, and a knack for using them gently. Then she shook her head. "Dr. Webster showed me how. I'll have to do it by myself eventually."

69

But Steve became insistent. "Let me hold the pup for you, anyway."

"All right," Jo conceded. "You can do that."

Together they walked back to the kitchen. Steve suddenly burst out laughing. "What's he got around his neck?"

To Jo the cocker looked anything but funny. "A collar," she said shortly. "So he won't scratch." While Steve knelt to examine the dog, Jo went to the sink and washed her hands. Then she came back with the bottle of eye drops in her hand and dropped to her knees beside him.

"Wait!" Steve said. "The light's bad here. I'll bring him over to the table."

He lifted the little dog, holding a supporting hand under his body. "There's no need to tremble," he told the cocker. "Jo's not going to hurt you."

His quiet voice and hands steadied Jo's nerves. As she stood beside the table and watched the cocker respond to Steve's reassurance, she was outwardly calm. When Steve nodded to her, she held the dropper steady above the injured eye and counted as she pressed the bulb. "One, two, three."

"Good girl."

Jo bent her head over the cocker, stroking an ear, and said, "See, that wasn't so bad, was it? And if it's going to help you get well . . ."

7

"EVERY THREE HOURS, day and night."

At eleven Jo managed the routine competently and alone, but at two o'clock in the morning the alarm clock's clamor was like the knell of doom. Shivering in the summer night, she forced herself to sit up in bed, pull on a robe, and swing her feet to the floor.

"Every three hours, day and night."

At five she was awake before the signal, watching the first pink threads of dawn appear in the eastern sky, hearing the familiar dirge of the mourning doves and the chirrups of some incorrigibly cheerful birds. At eight she was deep in exhausted sleep, and her mother turned off the alarm and smoothed the hair back from her daughter's forehead tenderly. "Jo. Jo, dear!"

Jo rolled over and buried her head in the pillow.

"It's eight o'clock, Jo."

Every three hours, day and night.

Was it only yesterday afternoon, Jo wondered as she went out to the kennels after breakfast, that the chatter of the girls at the swimming pool had seemed so important to her?

Now the memory of Steve's strong hands holding Sherry was more real, by far, than the episode on the raft. Gail Chartriss had become a shadowy figure of no consequence, the picnic planned for today forgotten. The sun beat down on Jo's head, and weariness made her eyelids heavy. Steve had been nice last night—sympathetic, almost tender. He hadn't said a critical word about her boarding kennel. On the other hand, he hadn't stayed around. If she weren't so tired, she supposed she would start wondering whether he had been on his way to see another girl, but even a question like that didn't seem to matter now.

Jo hitched up her jeans and rounded the corner of the hedge. Roger, in the end pen, barked joyfully when he saw her, whipping his long tail back and forth and hurling himself high against the wire.

"Down, Roger! Down, boy! There's a good fellow!" Jo thrust her hand through the fence, letting him lick her palm. She was glad to see the pup feeling so frolicsome, because he had been moping at intervals, as though he were provoked at being transferred to the kennels from the house.

Yet the Great Dane's arrant good health seemed an insult to the small cocker spaniel, who was still in the kitchen, lying drugged and mercifully quiet in his improvised bed. It was to Sherry that Jo's thoughts kept returning as she cleaned out Roger's pen and refilled his water pan, to Sherry and the fear that the eye might not heal.

Last night, after Steve had left and her mother had

returned from her fruitless errand to the village, Jo had written a letter to Mrs. Jeffrey Keene. She had described the cocker's condition and explained, at her mother's suggestion, that veterinary fees and drug costs would be added to the kennel bill.

Dissatisfied with the first draft, Jo had put it aside and written a second, to which she added impulsively:

"P.S. Sherry is a darling, so gentle and patient. I have him in the house in a special bed, and I'll do everything I possibly can to make sure he gets well!"

The other dogs seemed to equal Roger in high spirits this morning. All of them knew Jo by now, and wanted to jump up or nuzzle against her legs when she entered their pens.

She talked to them, calling each by name, trying not to discriminate between her favorites and the less attractive boarders. Bitsy, the fat cocker, seemed to be getting even fatter, and Jo made a mental note to cut down on her food and to see whether Mac, the thin Scottie, couldn't be persuaded to eat a little more.

But she fondled the dogs with a divided heart this morning. Sherry was her major concern, the healthy dogs in the pens merely her charges.

When the morning chores were finished, Jo went back to the house and walked down to the R.D. box with the letter to Mrs. Keene, hoping to catch the postman. The Redmond mail had already arrived, however, including two envelopes addressed in her dad's familiar handwriting.

One was for her mother, but the thicker of the two letters was for Jo, and she tore open the envelope impatiently as she walked back up the lane toward the house.

A card fell out as she unfolded the notepaper, and skittered across the lawn in the light breeze. Jo chased it, caught it with her foot, then plumped down on the grass where she was, anchoring the rest of the mail under one knee while she read her father's letter.

My darling daughter!

I have to put an exclamation point instead of a comma because I'm so proud of you I could burst. The Redmond Boarding Kennels. A fine-sounding name for a fine-sounding project!

To be honest, Jo, I had pictured you moping around the house this summer, disappointed that college will probably have to be put off. Then to get your enthusiastic, amusing letter—you can't imagine what a lift it has given me.

You tell Luke Webster he has my heartfelt thanks for backing you. I'll write him myself, by and by, but just now they're limiting my activity.

As to the business end of your project, I have a couple of ideas. In the bottom drawer of the desk there's an old card file you can salvage, unless Ricky's swiped it for his grasshopper collection or something. I've enclosed a suggested form you might use to include the information you'll need and want. As to how you'll make out your bills, I can cover that later.

My love and my congratulations. Good-by for now.

Dad.

Jo read the letter twice. Her father's confidence buoyed her flagging spirits. After all, she decided, one swallow doesn't make a summer. One unfortunate inci-

74

dent mustn't undermine her assurance.

Still sitting on the grass, Jo examined the card. Dad had done a very complete job. According to the system he suggested, she should list each dog's name, kennel number, the owner's name, address, and telephone number, Date In and Date Out. A space had been left for Remarks, which made Jo smile, because she knew that her father had in mind the endless requests for special treatment. She promised herself to start the card file at once. Tonight she would find time to make up forms for the dogs already in residence.

But the day proved busier than Jo had anticipated. The end of June was at hand, and last-minute reservations kept flocking in by phone. Uncle Doc was apparently doing a good advertising job.

By midafternoon Jo had filled fifteen of her dog pens for the first two weeks in July, and on her kennel chart there were reservations for several more boarders to arrive later in July or in early August.

Between answering the telephone, nursing Sherry, and fetching several cases of canned food from a supplier, Jo was kept on the run all day. Even her mother's help didn't ease the situation. She dropped into bed exhausted shortly after eight o'clock.

"I'll take care of the eleven o'clock drops," Mrs. Redmond insisted, ignoring her daughter's protests and resetting the alarm.

The house was pitch-black when the alarm went off at two A.M., and the scooting wind of a thunderstorm was whipping branches of wistaria vine against the kitchen windows when Jo stumbled downstairs. The yellow electric light flooded the sink and refrigerator with an antiseptic glow. Jo shivered in its glare.

Sherry, in his box, didn't even raise his head to blink, and Jo had to hold the lid back from the injured eye while she automatically counted the drops that made him wince away from her.

"Poor baby," she crooned.

Peril seemed to lurk in every corner of the house tonight, and the intermittent flash of lightning accentuated Jo's fears. When she knelt beside the spaniel she was full of anxiety and pity. Sherry was as important to her as Inky had been—as special as though he were no mere boarder but her very own dog.

She wondered if Uncle Doc felt this way about his patients. He couldn't! A veterinarian would have to develop a quality of mind that would protect him from overwhelming dismay if he couldn't save an animal's life.

She supposed the satisfactions of a doctor's life far outweighed the disappointments. For the first time she thought of veterinary medicine as something truly rewarding. She wondered how many years of study were required and if scholarships were offered to women.

A thunderclap put a period to Jo's drifting thoughts. Sherry was comfortable again, curled in a ball in his box. Rain was pounding against the roof as Jo tiptoed upstairs through the sleeping house, now dark, now eerie with flashing light. In bed again, she lay for a few minutes watching the convulsive shaking of the trees, silhouetted by the lightning outside her window.

A warm sensation of satisfaction crept through her

gradually. At least she was doing something constructive to try to save Sherry's sight. At least—

"What day's today?" Ricky asked his mother at breakfast the next morning, as he shoveled scrambled eggs rapidly into his mouth.

"Saturday."

"I mean what date?"

"The twenty-fifth of June."

"Oh!"

"Why, dear?"

"I just wondered, that's all."

Ricky turned to Jo. "How much have I earned on the money I gave the guy at the Dam?"

"Something over ten dollars, Rick. I'd have to get my book to be sure."

Ricky sighed. "It sure builds up slow."

Mrs. Redmond couldn't quench a smile. "Why don't you make a deal with Jo to work for an hour each morning? Then you'd be out of the red in two weeks."

"Would I?" Ricky looked surprised and pleased. He thought for a minute, then said, "Okay. I'll start today."

Jo looked doubtful. "There's only one big job to be done in the mornings."

"What's that?"

"Cleaning out the runs."

Ricky wrinkled his nose, then shrugged. "Work's work," he said jauntily, and shoved back his chair. "After the rain last night, it'll be a cinch today."

The rain last night had indeed given both the garden

and the kennels a clean, fresh look. The Paul Scarlet climber was bursting into bloom, and six more dogs were due to arrive during the day. Jo prepared their quarters, humming as she worked, because even Sherry seemed a little more alert this morning.

The first car came up the drive at nine o'clock, bearing a beautiful pair of Irish setters. Next came a Boston bull, then a springer spaniel, followed by a plush-coated Chesapeake Bay retriever named Felicity. Jo stuck her head in the kitchen door and reported to her mother, who was making strawberry jam.

"I'm getting quite a collection of breeds!"

A station wagon stopped at the foot of the lane, backed and pulled in. Jo crossed the grass to receive a collie who jumped down from the lowered tailgate with dainty feet. His ruff was so full, his sable and white coat so carefully brushed, that he might have stepped out of the pages of a picture book.

"Gee, Mom, here comes Lassie!" Jo heard Ricky say.

The owner of the collie, a squarish man in his late forties, looked toward the back of the house and smiled. "I'm complimented, and I'm sure Sandy is too," he told Jo. "Tell your little brother our dog can't lay claim to a movie contract, but that he is a champion."

Jo had no sooner delivered Sandy to his new quarters than the telephone rang. "It's for you, Josie," her mother called. "Ginny wants to talk to you."

"Jo!" Ginny said in some excitement. "I have good news. Gail's mother really is going to send you their poodle to board while they're away!"

"Well, that's nice. Business is business," Jo said, then

78

added, "I hope they make reservations soon. I'm almost full up."

"You are?" Ginny made no effort to conceal the astonishment in her voice. "I thought you were just getting started. I told Mrs. Chartriss I was sure there'd be plenty of room."

Jo appreciated Ginny's good intentions. "There was until this morning," she told her. "But now I have quite a bunch of boarders. You'll have to stop by and say hello."

"I will!" Ginny promised. "I've been meaning to get over, but somehow I've been so busy the last few days." Her voice trailed off apologetically.

You've been busy, sister! Jo felt like saying, but instead she laughed. "I know what you mean."

"Now, Jo, there's no use getting offended about Gail and Steve!" Ginny said in a scolding tone. "I didn't get her the date. Jane did. I just happened to be along on the party. It wasn't anything I could do anything about."

Offended? Gail and Steve? Jo was confused. "What are you talking about, Ginny?"

Then she realized that Ginny had leaped to the wrong conclusion, and had pulled a boner. Jo let her writhe on the other end of the wire for a few seconds, then said with elaborate casualness, "Look, darling, Steve is free, sane, and nearly nineteen. He's able to come and go as he pleases, you know."

"Oh, Josie," Ginny wailed, "I knew you'd be upset. And it's all too perfectly silly for words. We decided to go square dancing night before last, and Gail doesn't know many people around here yet, and you've been so busy, and Jane just happened to suggest—" She stopped, breathless.

Night before last. The night Steve had stopped by with the eye drops. That was why he hadn't stayed around. He had had a date with Gail Chartriss. Gail, with her pale-blond hair, her long fingernails, her sleek look of a well-groomed cat. Jo's mind flashed back to the quarrel she and Steve had had about the business, and she became aware, suddenly, that she was sitting Indian fashion on the floor in a pair of her father's discarded khaki pants, that her shoes were caked with mud, and that three nails on her left hand were torn back almost to the quick. Mrs. Truck!

"Ginny, look, you're in a completely unnecessary dither," Jo managed to say with creditable coolness. "I've got to go now. I really must! But for heaven's sake, don't spread it all over town that I'm jealous of Gail Chartriss, because I'm not."

8

PERHAPS IT WASN'T jealousy, but something made Jo's heart do a peculiar flip when, that same afternoon, she saw Gail's yellow car parked in front of Brett's Pharmacy next to the Rabbit.

Steve, his long legs crossed, his arms folded on the door, was so engrossed in conversation that he didn't notice Jo as she drove by. There was a vacant parking space two doors down, but Jo went on to the next block before she pulled in, then did her errand in a chain drugstore instead of in Brett's.

That night she spent a long time manicuring her nails. The result was not exactly glamorous, but somehow it was a step in the right direction. She creamed her face before she went to bed, and washed her hair. When her mother stopped in the bedroom door to say good night, she lifted her eyebrows in mild surprise. "Is there something special happening tomorrow?"

"No. Just trying to keep up appearances."

Mrs. Redmond smiled. "You've never looked better, honey, than you do this summer," she said loyally.

"Those few freckles across the bridge of your nose are very becoming, you know."

The next morning, when Jo again drove into the village to replenish her supply of dog biscuit, which she had learned to buy in twenty-five-pound sacks, she avoided Brett's as assiduously as she had on the previous day. She did, however, notice that the Rabbit was not around.

It was nearly eleven o'clock when Jo reached home, and as she turned into the lane she immediately recognized a yellow car parked by the garage. What, she wondered, could Gail want of her? She checked her appearance quickly in the rearview mirror, then pulled up behind the other car and got out.

Gail wasn't at the wheel. A black man in a white jacket was trying to disentangle two leashes, without much success.

"Keep quiet, now. Wait a minute! Keep quiet," Jo heard him mumbling. "Sit! There's a girl."

A green leather lead attached to the harness worn by a large black poodle, clipped in the stylish French fashion, had become snarled with a piece of clothesline knotted around the neck of a young beagle. The contrast between the two dogs, one almost ridiculously elegant, and the other looking like a typical country hound, was so amusing that Jo grinned broadly.

"Is there anything I can do to help?"

The man, so absorbed that he hadn't heard Jo's car, looked up with a start. "Thank you, miss. I'll manage."

Jo waited, wondering whether this were Gail's car after all, or perhaps one just like it. The man talked to the dogs as he worked, trying to calm the poodle, who seemed highly nervous. Jo stood by silently, admiring the soft cadence of his voice. Finally he straightened with a sigh of relief. "There!"

Briskly, now, he got the dogs down to the ground and took a white envelope from the pocket of his coat. "I need to see Miss Josephine Redmond," he said.

"I'm Miss Redmond."

"Oh. Beggin' your pardon, miss. This here's from Mrs. Chartriss. She said I was to give it to you when I delivered the dogs." He held out the envelope.

Jo took it with some hesitation. "When you delivered the dogs?" she repeated, frowning. "You mean—?"

The girl's apparent confusion made the young man look around in some concern. The kennels were, of course, concealed by the six-foot hedge, and he asked. "This is the place that takes dogs to board, isn't it?"

"Yes," Jo admitted. "But it is customary to call and make a reservation." She was rather proud of that sentence. It sounded firm and businesslike.

The man looked apologetic. "I'm sorry, miss. Maybe my madam didn't understand. She just said I was to bring the dogs and give you the note." He nodded to the envelope Jo was absently tapping against the back of her left hand.

The beagle, on her length of clothesline, had busied herself running around her escort's legs, so that the houseman had to bend down and unwind the rope, while he held the poodle at arm's length. Immediately the little hound started to wag her tail with a circular motion and lap joyfully at the man's face.

"Now, Suze! Suzy! Leave me be!" The reprimand was gentle.

Jo smiled as she pulled the folded sheet of notepaper out of the unsealed envelope. Whatever she might think of Gail Chartriss, and suspect of her family, the houseman was nice.

In a bold backhand Mrs. Chartriss had written:

My dear Miss Redmond,
   Richard is bringing our French poodle, Trinket, to stay with you until our return from Maine the first of August. Trinket is a valuable poodle, and will need to be combed and brushed daily. Kindly use her own equipment, which accompanies her, along with her feeding bowl and bed. Her diet should be as follows:
   Morning: 2 scrambled eggs.
   Evening: 1 pound lean beef, lightly cooked.
   She should be exercised for an hour daily, and should be kept from any contact whatsoever with other occupants of your kennels.
                    Very truly yours,
                    Abigail (Mrs. Henry B.) Chartriss.

P.S. The beagle is a stray who has been annoying us for the past several days. Please arrange with either the S.P.C.A. or a local veterinary to have her destroyed, and if there is a charge, forward the bill to me at the address given. Also report to me weekly on Trinket's condition.

For the second time Jo reread the postscript, allowing its full, presumptuous, cold-blooded meaning to penetrate her mind. Then her glance dropped to the young beagle, who was sitting back on her haunches now, looking from Jo to Richard and back to Jo again with appealing brown eyes. Jo wasn't familiar with beagles as a breed. It was the first time she had ever encountered that special, pleading look which distinguishes the smallest of the hounds.

Abruptly she raised her eyes to meet the houseman's. "I'll have to call Mrs. Chartriss at once," she said. "I can't possibly do as she asks."

About to turn on her heel and go up to the house, Jo was stopped by Richard's worried voice. "But Mrs. Chartriss isn't at home, miss," he explained, disquieted. "The whole family is gone to Maine and the house is locked up. I was told to bring you the dogs and then go off on vacation myself."

"You mean she had the nerve—?" Fury welled, hot and choking, to Jo's throat. Then she checked herself. After all, she doubted that the mild-mannered young man had been told what his mistress had written on the expensive notepaper she held in her hand.

Right now he stood beside the car, fumbling with the leashes, looking both confused and disturbed. "I'm sorry, miss, if something is wrong. Mrs. Chartriss just said—"

"That's all right." Jo forced a smile. "I didn't realize the situation. I'll take care of the dogs."

Richard looked relieved. "I'll get Trinket's stuff," he said, and brought a wicker basket and a feeding bowl from the rear of the car, then followed Jo back to the kennels, explaining as he walked along that the poodle was apt to be suspicious of strangers.

"She's pretty high-strung," he explained. "Maybe that's the way with these fancy-bred dogs. But little Suzy

Beagle now, she's as friendly as they come. Jus' turned up at the back door one morning, and been hangin' around ever since."

Jo looked down at the small tricolor hound, who was trotting along with a springy step, tail high, nose twitching at the scent of so many other dogs. "You named her?" she asked.

"Yes'm," Richard said proudly. "Mrs. Chartriss didn't rightly take to Suzy, off at the start. Tell the truth, I was mighty relieved when I found she was sending her to the kennel along with Trinket. I was afraid she might be thinking of turning her over to the dogcatchers."

His whole face was so alight with relief that Jo didn't have the heart to tell him what his mistress did have in mind. She put Trinket into the pen next to a Boston bull, who immediately struck up an acquaintance by sniffing at the poodle through the wire. The stray beagle went into the kennel adjoining the fat cocker spaniel's.

"This is Bitsy, Suzy Beagle," Jo introduced them. "You girls get to know each other now."

Suzy responded by a wild wagging of her entire rear end, and the cocker waddled inquisitively to the fence and peered at her next-door neighbor. Richard stood by looking satisfied. "I can see you like dogs," he said. "Some folks is doggy and some isn't."

If there was unspoken criticism of the Chartriss family behind this remark, Jo chose to ignore it. She went back with the young man to the drive, wished him a pleasant vacation, and said good-by.

But as Richard turned out of the lane, Jo was racing into the house, the screen door to the kitchen slamming behind her. "Mother!" she called. "Mother!"

Then she remembered that it was her mother's morning to do volunteer work at Bryn Mawr Hospital. She had driven down with one of her friends, doubtless leaving just a few minutes before Jo arrived home. Having no one in whom to confide, Jo sat down and read the letter from Mrs. Chartriss again.

The arrogance of the wording, the heartlessness of the postscript, struck her again. Here was a woman who hadn't even bothered to check, personally, on the boarding kennel to which she was entrusting a valuable dog. Yet she demanded special treatment for her pet as though it were her due! At the same time she quite casually turned over to a complete stranger a disagreeable job which she didn't care to bother with herself. Sitting on one corner of the kitchen table, Jo bit her lip and fumed.

She wished she could tell Ginny the story over the telephone. But Ginny, as a friend of Gail's, might not understand. She thought of calling Uncle Doc, then reconsidered. With his tougher, masculine point of view, and his long experience in the kennel business, he would probably tell her, "You get all kinds in this game. Some clients are impossible, but what can you do?"

The thought of the young beagle, waiting out in the pen with such unsuspecting docility, made Jo's breath come in quick jerks. Then Sherry turned in bed and attracted her attention. She knelt by the box and stroked the little dog for a few minutes. "I'd better check on your medicine," she told him. "You may be running low."

Inside the kitchen cupboard there was a note propped against the bottle of eye drops. "Jo," it said, "Called Luke and he has ordered more from Brett's. Should be here by eleven. Mother."

Jo's stomach felt like a deflated balloon. A prescription from Brett's meant an encounter with Steve, just about the last straw.

Glancing at the clock, the hands of which stood at ten thirty, Jo manufactured an excuse to get away from the house. Roger had been moping for the past couple of days and she wanted to give him a turn in the exercise yard, which had been converted from Ricky's corral by the simple process of mowing the grass.

The minute the Dane was set free his whole demeanor changed. He gamboled about the larger space with puppy playfulness, almost knocking Jo down in his enthusiasm, and giving her cheek great swipes with his tongue.

If Steve finds nobody around the house, Jo reasoned, he'll leave the prescription on the porch. She would give him even a little longer than the half hour before eleven. It wouldn't matter if Sherry got his drops a few minutes late.

But when she had returned Roger to his pen and had given fresh water to the dogs who needed it, there was no longer an excuse for lingering at the kennels. If the Rabbit had come up the drive, she hadn't heard it. Still, it must be well past the hour.

No package was to be found on either the front porch or the back when Jo looked, yet the time was eleven twenty. She held the almost empty bottle of medicine up to the light, calculated the probable dosage remaining, and decided to give Sherry the drop or two left, rather than take the chance of waiting for the delivery of the new supply.

A moment later a voice at the kitchen door called a cheery hello, and Jo turned with a start. "I didn't hear you come up," she stammered.

Steve stepped over the sill. "Didn't you?" He looked especially debonair this morning, in a navy-blue knit shirt and chinos. His eyes were as bantering as the tone of his voice.

"No." The monosyllable sounded flat and stupid.

"Should I yodel or something on approach?" He held out a package. "Won't you be needing this?"

"I could use it," Jo admitted. "I'm a little short."

"Here," offered Steve. "I'll bring the dog over to the table."

As Jo extracted the bottle from its cardboard container he picked up Sherry, who blinked at him with a trusting brown eye. "Seems to me I'm always holding something for you," he said lightly. "Sometimes a dog, sometimes a bottle of—"

"But never my hand!" Jo tried to match the badinage in his tone, but somehow missed. It sounded more like raillery, sarcastic and bitter.

"Well!"

Jo blushed hotly.

Steve was looking at her in amusement. "Is that an invitation or a threat?"

"Neither," muttered Jo, without meeting his eyes. "I was just trying to be funny, and missed."

"What's wrong, Jo? You've got the jitters this morning." His eyes were sober and questioning now.

Jo realized that her fingers were trembling as she counted out the eye drops.

"I don't know—or rather, I do too." But she couldn't tell him about the beagle. "I—I just can't talk about it, please. Anyway, it's time for me to change the dressing on Sherry's back."

"Okay. Let me help. You hold him this time." It wasn't a suggestion. It was an order. Jo meekly did as she was told.

She knew she would have fumbled from nervousness, but Steve was deft. The spaniel didn't squirm or cry and lay looking up at his new doctor patiently.

"Think the eye seems any better?" Steve asked.

"I don't know."

Jo gathered up the smelly discarded bandages while Steve carried Sherry back to his bed. "Thanks, Steve," she said without turning from the sink.

"Nothing to it. Call Dr. Chance any time."

Was there a rueful note in his reply? Jo turned to face him, but he was already at the door.

"Be seein' you."

9

AFTER STEVE had left, Jo sat on the back porch steps with her chin in her hands, feeling thoroughly miserable.

She was annoyed at Steve, humiliated by the stupid retort she had made, angry at Mrs. Chartriss, and worried about Sherry. Emotionally, she felt battered.

She could tell herself, when Steve was out of sight, that it didn't matter to her whether he dated Gail or any other girl, but when he was with her there was an undeniable attraction, a pull that made her anxious and self-conscious. From now on she had better watch her words with Steve.

Now that Gail had gone to Maine, would he be calling her up again? Or had her business venture put her on his blacklist? If he wanted to be petty, let him! But Jo wished he hadn't left so abruptly. She wished their friendship were back on the former, casual basis which had been so comfortable and pleasant. She wished everything hadn't suddenly become difficult!

If only she could talk to someone about the way she felt! All during high school there had been Ginny in whom to confide, but even Ginny had become a stranger. For the first time Jo was aware of the aloneness of growing up, and it terrified her.

Besides being worried about her personal relationships and about Sherry and the forsaken little beagle, there were all sorts of other kennel problems to think about. Roger should have more exercise if he was to be kept fit. Pogo, the springer spaniel who had arrived a couple of days ago, steadfastly refused to eat. He must be cajoled into cooperation somehow—but how? Wrinkles, a little brown dachshund, was brooding in a corner of his pen, as desolate as a small boy sent unwillingly to boarding school. Uncle Doc had warned Jo that some dogs, accustomed to living in the bosom of a family, were like that. They needed extra affection and care to help them make the adjustment to kennel life.

Jo sighed and got up. She might as well go out to Wrinkles right away and play with him for a while. She tried to put the beagle out of her mind as she sat on the grass in the big exercise pen, throwing a ball for Wrinkles to retrieve in a short-legged flurry. But her thoughts kept returning to the other little dog.

The sight of the length of clothesline hanging to the right of the beagle's pen door made her seem doubly forlorn. Every paying boarder had his special leash, but not Suzy. Like an unwanted child, the abandoned dog was infinitely pathetic. After Jo had returned Wrinkles to his own run, she made a sudden decision. Opening the gate she called Suzy out.

"You stay with me for today," she invited. "You're the only dog in the place I dare let run. Nobody cares what

92

happens to you, except me."

The beagle was delighted to follow Jo back to the house and curl up beside her while she filled out cards for the dogs who had arrived during the past two days. She lay with her head on Jo's foot and looked up at her intermittently, perfectly content.

After a while Jo put aside her pen and leaned down to stroke the dog's smooth, caramel-colored head. "You must have come from somewhere," she mused aloud. "I wonder if they bothered to advertise." The past two editions of the local weekly were around the house somewhere. Jo looked them up and scanned the Lost and Found section, but neither a missing beagle nor a found beagle was reported.

"It's high time," Jo told Suzy, "that something is done about this."

She telephoned the police station first, and asked if any inquiries about a young beagle had come in there.

The sergeant at the desk was not busy at the moment and inclined to be helpful. "Got a boy who's lost a mutt with a gimpy leg, and a woman whose pet Pekingese has wandered off, but nobody checking on a beagle. Let me have your phone number and I'll give you a call, just in case."

Jo didn't have much hope that she would hear from him. She composed a short ad and phoned it in to the newspaper, arranging to have it placed in the forthcoming issue and billed, extravagantly, to her.

By the time her mother arrived home at noon Jo felt that she had taken some positive action, but her indignation at Mrs. Chartriss hadn't abated one bit. She immediately handed the note to her mother to read.

Mrs. Redmond's reaction wasn't quite what Jo had expected. She read the letter carefully, then raised her eyebrows and shook her head. But she had no solution to the problem. This was Jo's job—Jo's individual concern. Her attitude was sympathetic, but she merely said, "I hope you can work something out."

In the early afternoon Ginny stopped by to see what claimed her friend's attention so exclusively.

Jo was out in the exercise pen, working with Roger, and having considerable success in making him come to her on command. The big dog needed a good run daily, and Jo had just about decided to take him walking in the woods, letting him off the leash when they were safely away from the main road. A real gambol might cure his despondency, and she was pretty sure she had him under control. Again and again he trotted up at her whistle, eyes eloquent, tail wagging, telling her, dog fashion, that he understood.

The minute Ginny rounded the corner of the hedge the boarders greeted her according to their fashion, with barks, shrill yaps, and frantic pawing and jumping at the restraining wire.

Ginny put her hands over her ears, laughing, and ran the length of the walk between the kennels. Jo met her at the gate.

"You're a stranger," she explained, shouting above the uproar. "Dogs are both curious and gossipy, just like a crowd of kids."

In a few minutes the animals quieted, and Jo led Ginny from pen to pen, speaking to her charges by name, and giving a capsule description of each. Only Trinket, the French poodle, was unresponsive. She seemed to be upset by the clamor, and cowered in the middle of her pen, tongue lolling, forelegs trembling. When Jo opened the gate and called her name she backed away and snarled.

"She isn't very friendly, even at home," Ginny murmured.

"That's odd. She seemed happy enough with Richard, the Chartriss' houseman."

"Oh, she likes Richard," Ginny hastened to add. "He takes care of her."

"What about Gail and Mrs. Chartriss? Don't they ever make a fuss over her?"

"Not often." Ginny shook her head. "They treat her like a piece of bric-a-brac, something that's just around to lend atmosphere."

Jo nodded slowly.

"Not that they're unkind."

"Of course not." However, there was no ring of conviction in Jo's voice. She wondered why people without any special love for dogs bothered to own one—particularly a French poodle clipped to make her look like a circus performer.

Jo herself had never actively disliked a dog in her life, yet she felt no warmth for Trinket. Her absurd hairdo and her fidgety disposition made her seem singularly unattractive. Moving on past the poodle's pen, Jo made a mental note to try to win her over when she had more time.

Restraining her natural inclination to confide in a close friend, Jo didn't tell Ginny about the note from Mrs.

Chartriss concerning the beagle. Suzy was so quiet and so inconspicuous, trotting along at Jo's heels or lying contentedly in the shade on the back porch, that Ginny scarcely noticed her, except to say, "That looks like the pup who's been hanging around our neighborhood this last week or so." She was more interested in the business end of Jo's venture than in the dogs themselves.

"You know, Josie," she said as she accepted a glass of ginger ale and sank down in one of the garden chairs under the apple tree, "you ought to do quite well!" There was new respect in her voice as she added, "It must be an awful lot of work, but I bet it will pay. If you clear fifty percent—"

"I'll do better than that," Jo promised.

"Then maybe you'll be able to room with me after all!"

But Jo shook her head. "Not this year."

Ginny sighed and leaned her head against the back of the chair. "I'm going to miss you."

Jo felt the beagle's hard body push against her bare legs and dropped one hand to be caressed by a warm, wet tongue. "I'm going to miss you too." She said to Ginny impulsively, "I do already."

"Why, Jo, what do you mean?"

"I'm not sure, exactly," Jo confessed, thinking slowly and aloud. "I just feel as though the end of high school is like the end of a sentence. With a period after it. We'll go on, all of us, and do different things, but it will never be the same again."

Ginny wriggled and frowned. "I know we haven't seen much of each other lately, but you've been so busy—" She paused.

96

"I know. I wasn't implying anything. I was just thinking out loud."

Ginny put her half-empty glass of ginger ale on the grass beside her chair. "Why don't you come swimming with me? My suit's in the car."

Jo almost said yes, then thought better of it. "Some other day." She wanted to walk the Dane, and there would be Sherry's drops at five o'clock.

"How about the Phoenixville Fair tomorrow night? The gang thought it would be a bright idea to go, and Chuck said he was going to ask you."

"Chuck?"

Ginny nodded. "Or did Steve—?" She broke off abruptly.

Jo made it easy for her. She shook her head and chuckled. "Steve hasn't been around much lately. He calls me Mrs. Truck."

"He doesn't!" Ginny sounded properly indignant.

"Not really."

"Then he may phone you yet."

"I doubt it. He was here just before lunch."

"Here? Why?"

"With some medicine for a sick cocker."

"Oh."

Jo sighed. "In any event, I couldn't go off for a whole evening," she said. She explained about Sherry and her three-hour routine.

Ginny stood up. "Maybe your mother would take over," she proposed. "I'm sure Chuck will call you, and it will be such fun—a regular country fair with a ferris wheel and everything!"

Chuck did call, just a few minutes after Ginny left, but Jo said, "I'm sorry, Chuck. I can't."

"Oh, come on!" Chuck urged. "Ginny and Steve and everybody'll be going. We'll have a ball."

"I'd love it, but don't you remember—I'm sitting up with a sick pup."

"Okay, I won't push it. Some other time?"

"Why sure!" replied Jo, and meant it.

Slowly, after she had put down the telephone, she walked back to the kennels and got Roger, then started off across the fields to the woods. "Ginny and Steve and everybody," Chuck had said. She wondered who Steve's girl would be, now that Gail had gone to Maine. And she wondered whether, if Gail had stayed home, he would be seeing more of her. Unfastening Roger's leash, she set the big dog free. He bounded away across the field, then circled back to her with puppy enthusiasm.

"This is just what you need!" she told him, fondling his smooth head. "We'll do this often for the rest of the time you're here."

The shelter of the trees was welcome after the searing sun of early July. Jo's sneakers crunched on the pine needles and rattled the dried leaves. Roger, intrigued by the new smells of the woodland, cavorted around Jo in widening circles, all of his lassitude gone with a taste of freedom. Jo made little rushes at him and he bounded back and away from her, but when she sobered and called to see if her training would prove effective, he came at once on command.

Keeping the Dane within sight, Jo walked down a winding path that led through laurel and wild azalea to a

98

stream that led eventually to the Dam. It was flanked on one side by a meadow, on the other by the woods through which she had just come. Not a house was in sight. Only a rough footbridge across the brook reminded her that civilization was not far away.

In November gunners crossed this bridge, and in April schoolchildren rode their bicycles out from Wayne and followed the path through the woods in search of yellow violets.

Jo pulled off her sneakers and sat down on the edge of the worn planks, kicking her feet through the water. Roger slid down the bank on awkward puppy paws, panting for a drink, then sniffed along the stream experimentally. Jo watched him, half-smiling because she felt more at peace than she had all day. Then she turned to lie at full length on her stomach and cradle her head in her folded arms.

Once, in the spring, she remembered having come here with Steve, on a Saturday afternoon when the buds on the dogwood were just opening. Commencement had been very close and they had felt buoyed up, as full of sap as the leafing trees.

There had been spring beauties in the woods and Jo had found a stand of mayflowers along the brook. They had talked about graduation and college, and then they had talked about the years that were past—the long years that grown-ups always called the best years of their lives. Jo could close her eyes and see the sweater Steve had worn that day, an old brown crew-neck job with the elbows unraveling. He had looked very boyish, yet the way he had talked about his hopes of going to college and then to medical school had sounded very grown-up.

Miles away, in the distance that separated suburbs from the open country, a train whistle moaned. Then, aside from the shrill of a jay and the lazy gurgle of the water, it was quiet by the brook. Jo raised her head to look for Roger, then propped herself on one elbow. He was at the top of the slope staring intently into the woods.

One moment he was standing stock-still, the next he was frolicking in and out of the trees as though he had discovered an imaginary playmate. He disappeared for a minute, but as long as Jo could hear the snapping of twigs and the rustle of leaves she wasn't worried. Roger so obviously felt the need of stretching his legs and exploring. This would do him worlds of good!

Then from the woods came the sound of light galloping, and Roger jumped out into the sunshine a hundred yards upstream, followed by—another Dane? Jo stifled a gasp. It was a fawn, lightly freckled, almost a yearling, who bounded down the slope after Roger, passing him and leaping the brook on swift, twinkling heels.

While Jo watched, breathless with astonishment, afraid to move a muscle for fear of alarming them, the young deer and the half-grown Dane played a mad game of tag in and out of the woods and across the winding brook.

The fawn was so delicate, all eyes and ears and untamed grace, that he made the dog seem clumsy by comparison, but they were almost exactly the same color and height. Gradually, in their chase, they came a little closer to Jo, until a light breeze carried her scent toward them and the fawn stopped suddenly, quivering, his tail erect, his nose twitching.

100

For a memorable instant he was silhouetted against the sun. Then he kicked up his heels and was off, and this time Roger seemed to understand that he couldn't follow. Breathless, the puppy came back and sank down on the bridge beside Jo, tongue lolling, eyes and ears alert. Jo didn't speak to the dog, just put out her hand and stroked his back. After a while she got up and started home, with the Dane following docilely. But she noticed that now and then he stopped and listened, as though he were hoping his playmate would return.

10

RICKY, WHEN HE HEARD the story at dinnertime, was almost as big-eyed as the fawn. He went out to the kennels and stood in front of Roger's pen, considering the Dane with new respect. To Jo he said, "I wish he could talk."

Jo smiled gently. "I wonder how many people have said that!"

"Huh?"

"Have wished that a dog could talk."

"Oh."

"Some almost seem to."

"Yeah."

Embarrassed, Ricky walked away to phone Toby and tell him about the fawn. "Gee, I wish I could've seen him!" Jo heard him sigh into the mouthpiece as she entered the house. "I only saw a deer once in these woods around here."

He must have heard the back door slam, because when Jo walked through to the hall to ask her brother a question about his kennel chores he had disappeared—simply faded away.

Jo shook her head in mock despair, but didn't bother to chase him, as she might have done a few weeks before. She went to the kitchen to doctor Sherry, and found Suzy Beagle sitting by the cocker's box.

Jo stopped in the doorway. Suzy was sitting very straight on her haunches, tail wagging in an arc on the linoleum, ears cocked, eyes bright. Obviously trying to arouse the cocker's interest, she was making a small, calling sound—between a cry and a yelp—in the back of her throat.

The spaniel raised his head, to Jo's surprise, because heretofore he had ignored the beagle. Delighted, Suzy leaned forward and sniffed Sherry's stiff cardboard collar, then caressed his chops with her tongue. Sherry shook his head with unexpected vigor, and Suzy inched back, afraid that she had ventured too far. She turned and looked questioningly at Jo.

"That's all right, baby," Jo assured the little hound softly. "Sherry likes you. It's just that his eye bothers him."

Suzy wagged her tail and edged forward again, to lie down beside the cocker's box. There she stayed until Jo lifted the dog to the table. Then Suzy returned to Sherry's side again when he was put back in his bed.

That evening, while Jo wrote a letter to her father and made penciled calculations of her probable first month's earnings on a sheet of yellow paper, Suzy Beagle divided her attention between the kitchen and the living room. If she had wanted to do one thing to endear herself to Jo, she had happened on the perfect enterprise—helping to take care of Sherry, at the same time she was making sure, every few minutes, that her new protector was right on hand.

Bright and early the next morning, Uncle Doc stopped by to check that things were going along all right. When he examined the cocker's eye he seemed encouraged. "Take him off the drops after today," he ordered, then made small grunts of approval as he examined the wound on Sherry's back. "This dog's coming along fine."

He went to the kennels and complimented Jo on their appearance. "Fine-looking lot of boarders you've got too," he said, patting her shoulder.

Jo grinned up at him. "All except the poodle," she retorted. "Did you ever see such an absurd-looking creature in your life?"

The veterinarian went over to Trinket's pen and whistled. The Chartriss dog's ears rose at once, but she didn't come to the gate.

"Shy?"

"I guess so," Jo admitted. "Or nervous."

"She'll take some watching," Uncle Doc said. "These poodles are smart. Intelligent as they come."

Jo was unenthusiastic. "Then why don't they use them for Seeing Eye dogs, along with German shepherds?" she wanted to know.

"I'll tell you why." Luke Webster leaned on the gate and lighted a cigarette. "Because they're born clowns. They learn as quick as that!" He snapped his fingers.

"Twice as fast as any other breed. They'll perform perfectly nine times out of ten, but the tenth time they'll flub because they can't resist the impulse to show off. They make marvelous pets, though."

Jo frowned. "But the way that dog's clipped!"

Uncle Doc's eyes crinkled at the corners. "I know. I don't like show clipping either, but it takes all kinds to make a world."

Suzy Beagle began to rub against his legs, and he leaned down and pulled gently at one velvet ear. "How come the little rabbit hound's loose?"

"She's a stray," Jo explained. "I'm trying to find her owner." Somehow she didn't want to tell him about her disagreeable duty—not yet.

"She doesn't look as if she'd stray far from here," Uncle Doc commented as he walked back toward his car. The beagle was keeping so close to Jo's heels it was hard to avoid tripping over the compact body.

"She's adopted me," Jo said with a smile.

An hour later, just after the clock struck nine, Jo walked into the bank. Most of her savings were gone, used up on paint and supplies and food for the dogs, but in her hand she held several checks and a fair amount of cash in payment of board bills. From now on she would no longer be in the red! She felt more substantial and adult than ever before in her life.

In very little time she was walking out the front door to the glare of the street, a new bankbook with her name printed boldly across the front tucked into the pocket of her denim skirt.

Chuck was coming out of the barber shop across the street. "Hi!" he hailed her. "How's Barkers' Retreat doing?"

Jo laughed. "I'll bet you've been two days thinking that up!"

"For two days, it's good. Admit it."

Jo nodded. "I'll tell Mother. She'll especially appreciate it."

During the rest of the morning Jo was so busy she didn't have a chance to think about the Fair. This boarding kennel had developed into a full-time job, what with food preparation, paper work, and special care.

Right after lunch she bathed three dogs who were to be picked up by their owners in the late afternoon. Uncle Doc had told her that a well-run kennel always returned boarders bathed and tick-dipped. It made quite a bit of extra work for Jo, but there was a definite satisfaction in seeing a clean, antiseptic-smelling dog rush up to his master or mistress and be greeted appreciatively. Besides, one pleased customer brought in others.

The afternoon was humid and heavy. As Jo finished preparing the dogs' four o'clock dinner Ricky came in, swinging a pair of wet swimming trunks, and helped Jo carry the food containers out to the pens. The back of her open-necked shirt was drenched with perspiration, and she felt weary and a little disgruntled because of the heat.

"Why don't you take the car and go over to the Dam for half an hour?" Ricky suggested unexpectedly. "I'll exercise the dogs after they've eaten."

"Will you? Gosh, Rick, that would be great." Jo didn't need urging. She hurried back to the house, changed into her suit, and got away in a flash.

The crowd at the pool had thinned in the late afternoon, and none of Jo's friends were around, but the water felt cold and invigorating, and she swam across the pool and back again before she climbed the ladder to the raft.

There she lay flat on her back and tried to relax, but she still felt tense and jittery. She kept wondering who Steve might be taking to the Fair tonight, and wishing she were the girl. Because now there was no reason why she shouldn't go. She could have told Chuck this morning that the eye drops routine was ended, but he might have asked someone else in the meantime and, besides, she didn't really want to go with Chuck.

Finally she sighed, sat up, and pulled on her cap. She made a racing dive—really a rather good one!—from the edge of the raft, and swam to shore. Dinner was nearly ready when she reached home, but although lamb chops, peas, and a tossed salad was one of her favorite menus, she ate listlessly.

Her mother was a little anxious. "What's the matter, dear?"

"It's too hot to eat," Jo excused herself. "Even some of the dogs refused their dinners. That fat cocker, Bitsy, just lies on her side and pants. And when she won't eat it must be the weather."

Mrs. Redmond thought for a minute. "Ricky, are you going to be around this evening?"

"Yup."

"Then let's go to the movies, Jo," her mother proposed. "You need a change of scene."

Jo agreed as much for her mother's sake as for her own.

"I think you've got a touch of cabin fever yourself. With Daddy away it must be pretty dull. Nobody to talk to except Rick and me."

"Hey!" said Ricky belligerently.

"I suppose you think you're perfectly fascinating?"

"Fascinating yourself," Ricky mumbled, unable to cope with such a question, then added, in an indistinguishable running together of words, "Maylbeexcused?"

Mrs. Redmond nodded. "But remember to stay around. You're in charge tonight."

Jo and her mother did the dishes with dispatch, so they could make the first show. The feature was not particularly entertaining, but they came out into the summer night feeling refreshed, and drove home slowly, eating ice-cream cones.

"I didn't check on the dogs before I left. I'd better do it now," Jo said conscientiously when they had shut the garage doors. She went into the house for her flashlight, and remembered that she had left it up in her bedroom. Ricky's radio was blaring. His light was on. But Ricky himself was lying at right angles across the bed, sound asleep.

Jo switched off the radio and the light, found her electric torch, and went back downstairs and out to the kennels, following its beam. Later she couldn't remember exactly when the presentiment of disaster struck her. It might have been as she ran down the back steps, or it might have been as she rounded the corner of the hedge, but she was definitely apprehensive before she turned the flashlight on the kennels themselves.

Most of the dogs were sleeping outdoors because of

the heat, sensibly scorning the confinement of their houses. Only Roger's run was empty, and Jo's sense of foreboding increased as she walked over and flashed her light inside his house.

The Great Dane was gone!

Automatically Jo tried the latch on the gate. It was fastened. Her chest felt tight and her throat was choked with alarm. The hot, oppressive night made her brain feel torpid and unready to face the calamity as a fact. She went inside the pen and made doubly sure that Roger was not there.

Then, disregarding the immediate barking of the other dogs, she started to call him.

"Roger! Roger!" She whistled, but her breath was shallow and weak. Anxiously, she ran back to the exercise pen and flashed her light over the turf. The Dane wasn't here either. She walked along the border of the property and peered into fields and into neighboring gardens, but there was no sign of the big, fawn-colored pup.

Finally she ran back to the house, feeling a little frantic. "Roger isn't in his pen," she called to her mother as she took the steps to the second floor two at a time. "I'd better wake Ricky. Maybe he knows something!"

Ricky's slender body was heavy with sleep, and his eyes opened feebly and closed again. "Roger's not in his pen!" Jo told him breathlessly. "Did you let him out?"

Ricky turned over and lay with head cradled on one bent elbow. " 'Course not," he murmured convincingly. "He was right here all evening. He must be somewhere around."

Almost as he said the words, he was asleep, and Jo

didn't have the heart to rouse him again. His conscience was so untroubled that he obviously knew nothing of the Dane's escape. The big pup, lonesome for companionship, must somehow have scrambled over the top of the fence.

Hurrying downstairs again, she appealed to her mother. "What am I going to do?"

Out of other experiences with lost dogs, in the years of Jo's childhood, Mrs. Redmond said promptly, "First of all, I'd call the police."

The sergeant on the desk was the same one to whom Jo had reported the acquisition of the beagle. He seemed more amused than concerned. "First you find a dog, then you lose one. That about makes it even, doesn't it, young lady? Why don't you call it quits?"

"This isn't my dog," Jo explained. "I run a boarding kennel."

"You do?" The cop's voice rose in astonishment. "Well, now look-a-here." Jo could hear a scratching sound as the sergeant probably reached for a pencil and pad. "Who does this lost dog belong to? Give me his name and description and I'll see what we can do."

Jo tried to marshal her thoughts. "His name is Roger. He belongs to the McCallums—the Peter McCallums—on Upper Gulph Road. He's wearing a collar and a license and a name tag, with the McCallums' telephone number on it, but they aren't home."

"Where are they?"

"In California."

"Well, young lady, I'd advise you to go over to the

McCallum place and see if the dog is there. He probably moved along back home."

"That's a good idea."

"One more thing. Is he vicious?"

"Roger? Heavens, no! He's a lamb." She added, informatively, "He's only a baby—well, maybe I should say a youngster—even if he does weigh more than a hundred pounds."

"Then a fellow could go right up to him without being afraid of getting bitten?"

"Of course!"

"Okay. Tell you what I'll do. I'll be calling my men in patrol cars in a little while and I'll tell 'em to keep an eye out. What's your telephone number, young lady, just in case?"

Jo gave it, and thanked the sergeant profusely. His matter-of-fact manner made her feel a little less distracted. She resolved to try to face this catastrophe calmly. Maybe she would have the Dane back within an hour!

After relaying the sergeant's suggestion to her mother, she got the car keys from their hook by the front door and drove over to the McCallum place, keeping a sharp lookout along the roads for Roger. The moon was hidden by clouds, and the darkness was deepening, although midnight was still two hours away.

Every few minutes Jo stopped and called, "Roger! Roger!" Such a foolish sort of name, hurled into the night.

But no Dane puppy gamboled up in response. The houses, sprawled behind their screening trees along the winding roads, seemed peculiarly silent this evening. After each vain attempt Jo accelerated and hurried on, even the noise of the motor a relief after the stillness.

The McCallum house had a half-moon drive leading to the front door through two iron gates supported by square stone pillars. Jo had never before driven into the grounds and she felt like an interloper as she approached the empty house.

Shrubs flanked the entrance, and old elms shaded the lawn. The tires of the car crunched noisily on the crushed stone of the driveway, and Jo pulled up rather warily, wishing she were not alone.

"Roger!" she called in a tremulous voice. "Roger! Here, boy!" Leaving the car, she walked around to the rear of the house, but nothing stirred. She felt compelled to try once more. "Roger! Roger!" Not even an echo responded. The dog had not come home.

Driving back, Jo chose a different route and went through the same procedure of stopping at intervals and calling, but though several dogs, guarding their owners' houses, barked upon hearing a strange voice in the night, none was the bark for which Jo was listening. Growing more discouraged by the moment, she drove on.

Was disaster bound to overtake her summer venture? First there had been Sherry's accident, then the disagreeable business of Mrs. Chartriss' note, now—worst of all! —a lost dog. How could she ever face the McCallums if Roger couldn't be found? And they would be home in less than a week.

Maybe Steve was right. Maybe she had been too impetuous, brash, overconfident, all the things that lead to trouble. After all, she was only seventeen.

Idling along at twenty miles an hour, hugging the side of the road and peering into the woodland that lined it for half a mile in this section, Jo became more and more upset.

She was so self-absorbed that she turned almost into the path of an approaching car as she reached the lane leading home. Brakes squealed and Steve's familiar voice yelled, "Hey!" then added, "Oh, it's you! What are you trying to do, get yourself killed?"

"I thought you were at the Phoenixville Fair," Jo stammered in surprise.

"I was," Steve replied. "It's over."

"What time is it?"

"Going on eleven. What are you doing roaming the roads at this hour?"

"One of my dogs got away. I've been looking for him."

Steve shut off the motor of his father's car and climbed out, strolling over to where Jo had stopped at the lane's entrance. He reached in to the dashboard, switched off the ignition, and said, "Any luck?"

Jo shook her head.

"Which dog?"

"The Dane puppy."

"The McCallums' pooch? Good grief, he's quite valuable, isn't he?"

"I guess."

Suddenly Jo felt that if Steve asked her one more question she'd burst into tears. She had been fighting to keep her voice level, her emotions under control, but she couldn't hold out much longer. She felt a desperate urge to get away—up to the house—by herself—anywhere but here.

"For Pete's sake, don't you know whether the dog's valuable or not?" Steve's brows were drawn together in a frown. His eyes forced Jo's to meet his.

"Oh, go away, will you!" Jo blurted out childishly. With brimming eyes she began to fumble for the ignition key, bent on flight.

Then, abruptly, she gave up. Turning in the seat so that Steve wouldn't see that she was crying, she tried to cover her tears with a camouflage of temper.

"Go away, go away, go away! Don't you think I'm worried enough?"

11

JO DIDN'T HEAR the car door open, but suddenly Steve was there beside her, patting her shoulder, although her head was down on the back of the seat, hidden by one folded arm.

"Jo! Why, Josie! I'm sorry." His voice was unexpectedly tender, and his hands were awkward but gentle as he tried to turn her toward him. "I never meant—"

Jo shook her head, but she couldn't speak. And she wouldn't look up.

Steve began to stroke the short curls up from the back of her neck, as though he were comforting a child. The humidity had made ringlets of her soft hair, and her neck was tense and hot under his hand.

"It's my fault, Jo. You scared me when you turned the car in front of me that way. I didn't realize you were so uptight. It's my fault, Jo."

Intended to be soothing, his voice had the opposite effect, and Jo found herself sobbing as she felt for a handkerchief in her pocket.

"Darn!" she said in a muffled voice.

"Here." Steve proffered a tissue.

Jo blew her nose vigorously and managed a thin smile. "I don't generally go to pieces this way."

Steve's arm, across the back of the seat, slipped down, and his hand tightened on her shoulder. "You're just overtired."

"I'm all right now," Jo told him, but she didn't pull away.

After a minute or so Steve said, in a calm, companionable voice, "Now tell me about the dog. I'll help you look for him. When did he get loose?"

It was a short story to tell, and Jo didn't elaborate on the details. Steve listened without comment, then immediately took charge. "We'd better check with your mother to see if the police have phoned in yet. They're your best bet."

Together, Jo and Steve went up to the house. "If we need a car, we'll use mine," Steve said, so Jo put hers away. Mrs. Redmond was just putting down the telephone receiver when they walked into the living room. "Oh, hello, Steve," she said casually, then turned to Jo.

"A Mrs. Wykoff on Route 252 has reported the presence of a large animal in her garden. It sounds like Roger, and the police are checking now." She smiled and shook her head. "The thought of Roger stalking around terrifying the countryside has its amusing aspects, you'll have to admit."

But to Jo her responsibility for the Great Dane overshadowed any humorous angle the situation might have. It was encouraging news, but she wouldn't feel really comfortable until the dog was back safely in his pen.

"Want to take a run over?" Steve invited. "I know where the Wykoffs live. In fact, since I've had this job at Brett's, I'm an authority on the subject of where practically anybody lives."

Feeling the need for action, Jo nodded her head.

"Is it all right, Mrs. Redmond?"

"Certainly, Steve. I'm glad you happened by. I don't like Josephine running about alone at night."

The police were flashing lights through the shrubbery on the Wykoffs' two acres when Steve pulled up alongside the hedge. Jo was out of the car in an instant.

"I'm Jo Redmond," she said. "Any luck?"

"Not yet, miss."

Jo and Steve joined in the search, but half an hour's work yielded nothing. The Wykoffs themselves were patient but sleepy, and after a time they excused themselves and went to bed. The police car drove off in one direction while Steve took Jo in another. He circled the roads around the Redmonds' house, driving at a snail's pace while Jo leaned out the side of the car and called Roger's name again and again.

"Better give up," he said finally. "You're getting hoarse."

Jo was reluctant to admit defeat. "I have a feeling we've got to find him tonight, if we're going to get him back at all."

"Why? He might turn up safe and sound in the morning," Steve said optimistically.

"He might," Jo agreed, "but on the other hand, in the

daylight, somebody may coax him into a car and make off with him. He's so friendly he'll go to anybody—anybody at all."

Steve could see the reasonableness of this prediction. He thought for a minute, then said, "My pop's electric lantern is in the car trunk. It has a thousand-foot beam that's really great. We can start at your house and work the surrounding country systematically. It's too hot to sleep, anyway."

Jo wasn't sure how her mother would greet this proposal, but when they told her the plan she made no objection.

Changing to jeans, Jo realized that her hands were trembling. The clouds had drifted past the moon now, and the countryside was illumined with a wan and eerie light. Looking for a brief moment from her bedroom window, Jo was reminded of a treasure hunt she had been on a year ago. It had been on a night like this, with the moon skittering in and out of the clouds, and Steve was her partner because she had happened to draw his name from the hat.

Now he was her partner again, but on serious business. Jo suggested that they each take one side of the road, but Steve insisted that she stay with him.

"I don't want to lose you too. Roger's enough for one night."

Talking in whispers, so they wouldn't arouse any light sleepers, the pair circled the houses on the road leading toward the Wykoff place. They peered under low-growing shrubs and into open garages, and when they came to a barn they gave it special attention, because Jo had noticed a barn on the McCallum place and had an idea Roger might find a similar one that felt like home.

Occasionally they would arouse a dog who howled a warning, making a shiver creep up Jo's spine. Familiar houses and the shapes of trees seemed different in the darkness, different and almost menacing. After an hour her feet began to drag, and her eyes were so heavy they kept shutting against her will.

"Want to quit?" Steve asked.

The question shocked her into wakefulness. "Not yet. Let's just rest a minute, if you don't mind."

They sat on a big flat stone on the edge of the road, and Jo put her chin in her cupped hands, balancing her elbows on her knees. To save the battery, Steve put out his lantern, and the darkness was like black velvet without its glow.

With strange formality Jo said, "This is very good of you, Steve."

"I don't mind."

"You must be dead tired, after working all day." Jo skipped any reference to the Fair.

"You worked all day too." A thought occurred to him. "Say, what about that sick cocker? Still on the eye drop jag?"

Jo shook her head. "Uncle Doc took him off them today."

"Today?" Steve sounded surprised. "Why, golly, Jo, then you could've—"

A rustling in the weedy growth along the edge of the road interrupted him. He reached for his light, and at the same moment Jo felt a wet nose nuzzle her ankle. She drew back with a start, then chuckled softly and reached out to gather a wriggling body into her lap.

"It's just Suzy Beagle," she explained, before Steve could find the switch to his lantern. "She must have been following us all along."

Steve groaned. "Another dog to keep track of?"

"Suzy won't be any trouble," Jo tried to explain. "She never leaves me." She leaned to rub her forehead against the beagle's ear. "She's my girl!"

"Well, she's not my girl," grumbled Steve ambiguously and stood up with sudden determination. "Come on. We might as well get on back."

"Back?" Jo was still reluctant. "There are only three more houses before the highway. Let's just finish this road."

So with dragging feet they went over the ground. Jo didn't dare call Roger's name, for fear of awakening a sleeping householder, but she whistled softly now and then. Accepted by Jo as part of the expedition, Suzy clung to her idol's heels, padding along on silent feet. Her nose twitched occasionally, and her tail rose at the scent of another dog or a rabbit, but she never strayed nor barked. She was as quiet as the night.

"Give up now?" asked Steve finally.

This time Jo nodded her weary head. "Okay, I give up."

They turned homeward, walking slowly. Not a car nor an animal sound disturbed the peace of the small hours before dawn.

Jo couldn't remember any other time when she had been so tired. Her back ached and her feet burned with weariness. She limped a little without realizing it and not even Steve's presence could keep discouragement from settling down upon her shoulders like a dragging weight.

She could see Roger in her mind's eye so clearly! The day he arrived, the first of her boarders . . . the expression in his eyes as he sat, strange and timid, in the middle of the living room floor . . . the nights he had spent at the foot of her bed before the kennels were finished . . . the pleading look he always gave her when she passed his pen.

"A Dane could get a good distance away in eight hours, if he really decided to travel," Steve was saying as he trudged along.

Jo shook her head. "I still can't think Roger would go far," she said. "He's just a pup, playful and loving. He's never seemed like a roamer to me."

"Maybe we'll find he's come home by the time we get there."

Jo shook her head again, but she didn't bother to reply. She was too tired.

Only Suzy Beagle seemed undiscouraged. Her tail carried high, her tricolor coat showing only patches of white in the night, she trotted along at Jo's heels. If it had only been Suzy who had strayed!

But to Jo's surprise her throat tightened at the thought. She felt disloyal to the little foundling, and stopped to give the beagle's head a quick pat.

The house was in sight now, and Jo saw that her mother had left the lamps in the living room lighted. Lagging behind Steve, she plodded up the slope of the drive.

"I'll just wait a minute, and see if there's any news." Steve sank down on the lowest of the porch steps while Jo went into the house. A note on the hall table was propped against a vase of roses.

"Have gone to bed. Call me if you need me. Police still on the job. Mother."

Jo was about to turn back to tell Steve when creaking floor boards made her turn toward the kitchen. Ricky was emerging from the door with a fat sandwich clutched in one hand.

"Hi," he greeted her. "What goes on?"

Jo retorted with another question. "What are you doing, running around the house in the middle of the night?"

Ricky looked mildly surprised. "It's almost morning. I was hungry." He regarded his sister with curiosity. "Why all the lights? Where have you been?"

Jo turned back toward the porch, the note in her hand. "Don't you remember?" she asked with a sigh. "I awakened you and told you. Roger's lost. He must have jumped the fence."

She shut the screen door softly behind her, careful not to make a noise that would arouse her mother. "No news," she told Steve, who turned and looked up at her from the bottom step.

Ricky, padding along in bare feet, his pajamas rumpled and twisted on his thin body, took a satisfying bite of his sandwich and considered the situation. "Have you been looking for that big pooch all night?" he asked with his mouth full.

"Sh!" Jo warned him. "Don't wake Mother."

Ricky came through the door to the porch, holding the

122

frame with his heel to keep it from banging. " 'Lo, Steve," he muttered without special surprise. "Have you?" he asked again.

"We have," Jo said, exhaustion making her irritable. "And so have the police, if you want to know."

Ricky looked interested. "The cops? Gee!"

Steve had to smile. Suzy Beagle, interpreting the grin as a signal, immediately went over and put her head between his knees, asking for affection. Ricky sat down on the top step, took another huge bite of his sandwich, and mumbled, "Where you been looking?"

"Just about everywhere," Jo replied. "And now Steve's got to get home for a couple of hours' sleep." She herself was propped against a pillar, hardly able to stand upright.

"Today's a working day for you too," Steve reminded her wryly.

Ricky was absorbed in thought. "Of course you went back to the woods?" he asked as Steve finished speaking.

"What woods?"

Ricky looked at Jo. "The woods where you found the fawn."

"Why should we go there?"

Her brother's eyes widened in astonishment. "Why, that's the first place I'd look," he said matter-of-factly. "Like you said, Roger had a lot of fun with the fawn. It's the only place you ever took him. If I was Roger, that's the place I'd go back to." He looked at Steve. "Wouldn't you?"

Jo straightened and snapped her fingers like a boy. "Steve, I think he's got something!"

The first thin, golden light of a summer sunrise was

touching the eastern sky as Jo and Steve sped across the lawn. The earth was turning from gray to lavender and Jo was filled with a wild feeling of exhilaration which drowned her physical weariness.

"Hey! Wait for me. I'll get into some clothes," Ricky called after them, but they didn't hear. Suzy Beagle, infected with some of the early morning madness, leaped at Jo's side, then raced on ahead and circled back.

As they entered the woods, Jo began to tell Steve about the fawn, trying to put into words the way she had felt when she watched the two young animals race down the slope and across the creek.

"I think I know what you mean," Steve said. "Remember the fawn—what was his name—in *The Yearling?*"

"Flag." Jo nodded. "That's right. Swift and untamed and light as a feather. I wonder, if Roger had been older, whether he would have attacked the deer."

Steve shrugged. "He'd never have been able to catch it."

For a while they walked along the woodland path in silence, the leaves and pine needles slipping under their shoes. It was still dark under the trees with only streaks of light reaching through the leaves.

"We came here once before, remember?" Steve asked.

Jo nodded, but didn't admit how well she remembered.

By the moment she was getting more excited. If only Ricky should prove to be right! Suzy, ahead of her, had her nose to the ground and was sniffing along as if she was following a scent. Could she have recognized the trail of the Dane, or was it only a rabbit or some other woodland creature who had scurried along this path?

Finally the meadow and the brook lay ahead. "Let's go softly," Jo proposed, but her pace quickened along with the beating of her heart. Ricky had to be right!

Abruptly, at the very fringe of the black woodland, she stopped. "There he is!" she said, just above a whisper, and her hand caught Steve's.

Suzy, nose to the ground, went racing down the meadow to the creek, and only when her forefeet touched the bridge was Roger aroused. He had been sleeping calmly, head on paws, at right angles across the rough wooden planks.

For a single instant, when he awakened, his ears pricked and he glanced across the field toward the far curve of trees where he had first met the fawn. Then he got up, stretched, wagged his tail at Suzy, and in response to Jo's whistle galloped toward his human friend.

12

"SEE, I TOLD YOU SO!" cried Ricky triumphantly when Jo and Steve arrived back at the house, walking the Dane between them. He had changed from pajamas to shorts, and was lying along the porch railing, waiting for them.

His shout awakened Mrs. Redmond, who hurried downstairs in her robe and slippers, as relieved as Jo at Roger's return.

"What you youngsters need is a good breakfast, with ham and two fried eggs," she said as she looked at their perspiration-streaked, heavy-eyed faces.

"Three," Steve corrected her with a grin.

"You go wash. I'll get them cooking," promised Mrs. Redmond, giving the boy's arm a friendly pat. "Jo, will you get some fresh towels?"

It seemed strange to Jo to have Steve follow her upstairs and stand in the hall waiting while she went to the linen closet. His continued presence had an early morning unreality, brought on by nerve strain and weariness. "Should you call home and tell your family you're here?" she asked, trying to sound commonplace.

"Later. They won't be up yet."

"Oh, of course. I forgot."

Jo went into her room and ran a comb through her hair while Steve was in the bathroom. Then, when she heard him go downstairs, she splashed water on her face and dried it vigorously with a towel. The friction brought a little color to her pale cheeks, making her look less tired. She washed her hands systematically, already beginning to wonder what she would do to keep Roger within bounds during the final few days of his stay.

From the kitchen came the pungent smell of coffee, and suddenly Jo was as hungry as Steve. Ricky and he were already at the kitchen table when she ran downstairs, with Suzy and Roger sitting on the linoleum along with Sherry, while Mrs. Redmond fried the eggs.

"You don't mean to tell me," Jo said to Ricky, "that you're going to eat again?"

"Why not?" asked Ricky, the sandwich he had devoured an hour earlier not even flicking his memory. "I'm starved!"

The two boys ate with absorption, and it seemed to Jo that Steve's warm companionship had dissolved with the return of daylight.

"It's going to be another hot day," she said with a stifled yawn.

"Yep," agreed Steve.

"A scorcher," Mrs. Redmond conceded, looking out the kitchen window at the sun.

"I like it hot," put in Ricky. "The water feels so good."

Everybody knew that he was speaking not of bathroom bathing, but of the pool.

Steve buttered his fourth piece of toast and looked across the table at Jo. "You'd better tie up Roger. Next time he takes a notion to jump the fence he may head in another direction and he won't be so easy to find."

Jo raised her eyebrows. "Easy?"

"It was me who really found him," boasted Ricky.

"It was I," his mother corrected.

Jo felt called upon to make a little speech of thanks. She wanted to tell Steve how much she appreciated his help, and she wanted to tell Ricky that he had saved the day, but she stumbled over the words when she tried to say them.

For some reason Steve seemed more embarrassed than pleased. "Forget it," he said as he pushed back his chair. "Thanks for the breakfast, Mrs. Redmond. I'd better be getting home. Dad'll want the car, and I need a shower and a change of clothes."

He scarcely looked at Jo as he said good-by, just walked past Ricky's chair and tousled his hair as he mumbled something.

Jo felt deflated. After Ricky too went outside, she sat on at the breakfast table and wondered what had happened. Suzy came over and rubbed against her legs, and Jo reached down and fondled her, speaking to the dog in order to keep her mother from noticing her dejection. "I'll give you a bath tomorrow. You need one awfully."

Mrs. Redmond poured her second cup of coffee. "Steve," she commented thoughtfully, "has developed into a very reliable sort of boy. I like him."

"He's apt to be moody," said Jo.

"Moody? I hadn't noticed it."

"Well, why should he close up like a clam at breakfast?" Jo asked. "All he seemed to want to do was gulp his food and get away."

Mrs. Redmond smiled. "After all, he has been up all night. That may have something to do with it."

Weariness was making Jo cross. "So have I."

Patiently Mrs. Redmond said, "He was helping you do your job. With that over, he was concentrating on his own responsibilities."

"He could at least have been civil," Jo muttered.

"I think he was sufficiently polite. This wasn't a high tea, at six in the morning." Mrs. Redmond smiled thoughtfully. "We should invite Steve to dinner some night."

Jo's chair scraped sharply as she pushed it back. "Oh, no!" she cried. "Oh, Mother, please!" She looked stricken. "You've got to promise me you won't do a thing like that!"

If Ricky hadn't come back to the kitchen just then, Mrs. Redmond might have argued the point, but for the second time in a few short hours Ricky saved the day.

"Jo," he said, rocking back and forth on his heels in a substantial, grown-up fashion, "if you'd like me to take charge today, I'll be glad to. I think you need some sleep."

Jo's mouth dropped open a full inch. Then intuition came to her rescue, with the realization that Ricky had followed Steve out to his car.

"Why, thanks, Rick," she said gravely. "That would be a big help, because I am pretty beat up."

Ricky nodded. "Sure. Girls can't take it like us fellows."

Jo bit her lip to keep from laughing. After all, it was she and not Ricky who had scoured the countryside last night. To cover her amusement, she said, "You know the routine?"

"Why, sure."

"Sherry can be moved out to one of the kennels today."

"Yep. Will do."

"And you'd better tie Roger securely to the gate of his pen." She sighed. "I'll have to think about getting some wire to cover the top, but I don't know that it's worthwhile, since he'll only be here a few days more."

"I'll take care of everything," Ricky said pompously. He started back to the kennels for Roger's leash with a self-confident stride, while Jo looked at her mother in amazement. She pretended to wipe her forehead with the tips of her fingers, and whispered, "Whew!"

"He's maturing noticeably this summer," Mrs. Redmond murmured.

"Cross your fingers. It may not last," Jo replied, skeptical.

Her mother's eyes twinkled. "I can remember the summer you were nine. Your father said the same thing about you."

"Touché!" Jo accepted the reprimand and came around the table to kiss her mother lightly. "Unless Ricky runs into a real snag, please let me sleep until noon."

"Until sundown if you like," Mrs. Redmond replied. "Ricky will simply adore being boss."

She was right. Ricky reveled in a new feeling of importance all morning, and if he used Tom Sawyer's technique in enlisting the assistance of Toby, only Mrs. Redmond knew. She felt so sorry for the gullible Toby that she invited him to lunch, and let the boys picnic on the lawn while Jo slept on undisturbed. Only the crack of thunder heralding an afternoon shower awakened her, and she rolled over and stretched, feeling sluggish but sufficiently rested to contemplate getting up.

Ten minutes later, standing under the bathtub shower, she washed her short hair. Then she dried it roughly with a towel, dressed from the skin out in clean clothes, and went downstairs.

The thundershower had cooled the earth only briefly, and the inside of the house, though darkened against the July heat, was still close and uncomfortable. Jo found her mother stretched out in a deck chair under the shadiest of the maples, reading her mail.

She looked up when Jo came across the lawn. "Hello, darling. Feeling better?"

"Much!"

Mrs. Redmond took some envelopes from the grass beside her chair and held them out. "You're the person who gets all the letters these days."

Jo riffled through them. "Business," she said, pride showing through her assumed indifference. "Oh! And a letter from Dad."

"I have one too," said her mother, going back to reading the closely written pages filled with familiar handwriting. For several minutes they were quiet and absorbed, Jo sitting Indian fashion on the grass, Mrs. Redmond relaxed in her chair, a soft smile touching the corners of her mouth.

"Dad seems in fine spirits!" Jo murmured.

"He does," her mother agreed. "He asks particularly about the dog business. You'll have to write him about Roger. It will make quite a tale."

"Tonight," Jo promised. "And I'll tell him about my finances. I'm doing all right."

She felt proud of herself and happier than she had been in weeks. Roger was safely back again, Suzy Beagle was chasing a chipmunk over by the perennial border, Ricky was being cooperative, and her mother was obviously cheered by Dad's news. If only something unforeseen didn't happen, the summer should roll along smoothly from here on.

With leisurely interest, Jo opened the rest of her mail. The owners of the red cocker, Sherry, were relieved that he was improving, and were not especially concerned about his doctor bills. Mrs. Chartriss had written to inquire in abrupt, undiplomatic terms about Trinket's welfare, and to ask what disposal had been made of the beagle.

Jo folded the letter hastily and tucked it back into its envelope. She promised herself to devote more time to Trinket, still shy and aloof, but the problem of the beagle she deliberately pushed to the back of her mind, as she had so many times before.

It was not until the following afternoon, at almost exactly the same hour, that she was forced to face it. She had put in a strenuous day, but her chores were finished. In addition to the usual routine, she had spent the better part of an hour making friends with Trinket, and was surprised at the poodle's intelligent response to a sincere effort on her part. Then, because she had promised her, Jo washed Suzy with a good dog soap, toweled her shining coat, and fastened her by a staked chain so that she could dry in the sun on the lawn.

"You look beautiful!" she told her, and stood admiring while the little dog wriggled in delight, her white legs and feet, her throat and the tip of her tail all gleaming in the sun. But when Jo walked away to sink down in a deck chair and cool off, the beagle fought frantically with the restraining chain, yelping with frustration until Jo came over and released her.

"All right. But stay there!" Jo made the little dog lie down on the grass. "Stay there!"

Suzy cowered, looking up at Jo with pleading eyes, but she didn't move. For fifteen minutes she lay in the sun, drying, until Jo whistled from her chair, and the beagle raced over to leap ecstatically on her lap and cover her neck and arms with damp kisses.

It was while they were playing that a truck lumbered into the drive and a middle-aged man in work clothes climbed down from the driver's seat.

Jo tumbled Suzy unceremoniously from her lap and stood up. She was just about to explain that her mother wasn't home when the man asked, "You the party that run the ad about the hound dog?"

Jo's heart began to beat with a quick rat-a-tat. Suddenly she began to wish that she had never contracted for that ad, and she was aware that Suzy Beagle, far from being her usual friendly self, was sitting on the far side of the deck chair with a definite air of suspicion in her eyes.

"Yes," Jo admitted hesitantly.

"I live over the hill a piece," said the man, indicating with a jerk of his head the direction of a small, ramshackle community on the outskirts of Wayne. "Seems like you picked up my dog, miss." He was looking past Jo toward Suzy. "Little old hound dogs is born wanderers, sometimes."

Jo's spontaneous reaction was one of mistrust. This beagle was no wanderer! Then she was assailed by a premonition of loss. But suppose this was the dog's owner? Suppose he had kept her tied up or had mistreated her, and she had simply fought free and run away? Even so, she could be required to turn Suzy over to him. The thought made her feel sick and weak.

But she kept her voice remarkably steady. "What was your dog's name?"

"Rip," the man said, and it told Jo nothing, because it could be a name for either a male or a female.

"And when was the dog lost?"

" 'Bout a month ago now."

Jo swallowed hard. The timing was right, and this increased her dismay. But she knew she mustn't show that she felt antagonistic. "Do you mind telling me your name, and a little about the dog, please?"

The claimant twisted an old felt hat in his hands. "My name's Howard Land," he said willingly enough. "This houn' dog was give me by people I used to work for." He added hurriedly, "They moved away."

"Do you know where they moved?"

"No, miss, I don't, but that's my dog, all right." Howard Land indicated Suzy, who was still crouching on the far side of the chair, and gave a peremptory whistle. Suzy trembled and hung her head, but she didn't budge.

Trying cajolery, Mr. Land crouched on the grass and snapped his fingers. "Here, girl. Here, Rip!"

Suzy lay down and put her head on her paws.

"Don't know the old man after a month, eh?" The fellow shrugged, and showed uneven, tobacco-stained teeth in a placating grin.

But Jo was only conscious that he had called the beagle "girl." It was conclusive that he at least knew her, and it made her feel even more heartsick and reluctant to give the little dog over to his hands.

"I've been calling her Suzy," Jo said when his wheedling failed. "Here, Suzy Beagle. Come here!"

Suzy came, but she came on her belly, crawling over the grass with her tail dragging and her eyes eloquent with fear.

Howard Land stood up. "Always was the hangdog type," he pronounced. "But there's no doubt she knows me."

There was no doubt in Jo's mind, either, that Suzy knew him, but she suddenly had a wild desire to stall for time. She couldn't—she simply couldn't!—give the defenseless little pup up without a fight.

"I—I've got to speak to Dr. Webster before you take her," she managed to stammer. "You see, the family that found the dog made me—and him—responsible, and I have to make sure it's all right to release her."

It was a garbled explanation, dreamed up on the spur of the moment, and didn't satisfy Howard Land, but Jo stuck to her guns. She would not give the dog up without the veterinarian's approval, she insisted. However, Mr.

Land could stop back tomorrow, if he liked.

After the man had reluctantly backed his truck down the lane, Jo sank down on the grass, weak-kneed, and gathered Suzy into her arms. "It would be better to put you to sleep," she confessed in a heartbroken murmur. "It would be better to have you destroyed than to give you back to that man!"

13

FIFTEEN MINUTES LATER Jo was on the telephone, pouring out her troubles to Uncle Doc. Her voice was shaky with emotion, but she managed to tell the whole story, from the time Richard had delivered Suzy, along with Trinket and the unfortunate note, to her encounter with Mr. Land.

Uncle Doc let Jo finish, then said briskly, "I know Land. He's done some work for me. It may be his beagle, all right, but I'd like to take a look at her before you turn the dog over to him."

"You've noticed her running around the place," Jo reminded him. "She's never tied up."

"I know. But I haven't paid much attention. Good grief, Josie, I see dozens of dogs every day!"

"She's awfully sweet," Jo murmured. "And gentle, and affectionate, and—"

"Okay, Jo. I said I'd stop by. Now just sit tight and relax till I get there, will you?"

"I'll try," Jo promised. But of course relaxing was out of the question. She paced fretfully up and down the front porch, Suzy right at her heels, and every endearing trait the beagle had ever exhibited began to haunt her—the way Suzy had immediately adopted her, the ardent eyes that begged to be let out of the pen, the feel of the beagle's cold nose in her palm as she sat exhausted on the stone by the roadside with Steve. She recalled, too, the sweet concern Suzy had felt for the ailing cocker.

Then, in a sickening flash, she thought of the abject fear in Suzy's eyes when she had looked up at Mr. Land. Oh, why had she ever placed that stupid ad in the paper?

A car stopped in the drive and Jo turned hopefully and started down the steps, but it wasn't Uncle Doc. It was Steve. He backed toward the garage, waved to Jo, and got out.

Jo started across the lawn, but Steve, instead of waiting for her, went around to the rear of the car and opened the trunk. He hauled out a bulky roll of chicken wire and dumped it unceremoniously on the grass at her feet.

"Here. This was in the garage and Pop said you could have it. You can use it to roof Roger's pen."

"Why, Steve, that's awfully nice of you!" Jo was surprised.

"Don't thank me. Thank my pop." Steve was brusque. He seemed embarrassed, anxious to get away. "Make sure you get it fastened down tight," he cautioned as he slid under the wheel once more. "Bye now. I've got things to do."

Jo would have liked to tell him about her new problem, and to have thanked him again for his all-night aid, but he was down the drive and out into the road on skidding tires before she managed to collect her wits.

While she was dragging the bulky roll of wire to the back of the garage the veterinarian drove up. Jo dropped her burden and hurried toward him, Suzy frisking in front of her.

"Oh, Uncle Doc, I'm so glad you've come!" she cried. "I'm in the most dreadful jam."

Uncle Doc put his arm around her shoulders and gave her a reassuring hug, then almost chuckled as he said, "There, there. Nothing can be quite that bad, Josie."

"It is, though," Jo retorted. "I can't let that man take Suzy back. I simply can't!"

The veterinarian looked down. "Is this the dog?"

"Yes."

Uncle Doc whistled. "Come here, Suze."

Suzy trotted up to him at once, tail wagging, head high, and Luke Webster stooped and cupped her muzzle in his palm. "Nice head."

"She's a darling," Jo said.

Uncle Doc walked over to the group of garden chairs, in the center of which stood a low table. He picked the beagle up gently and stood her in front of him, placing her forelegs just so and holding her head and tail so that he could see her points. "Good stance."

Jo nodded, ready to agree with anything that sounded like praise of Suzy. Uncle Doc began to run a hand over her back, then frowned thoughtfully. "She's marked like a Shortridge beagle," he muttered half to Jo, half to himself. "Where did Land claim he picked her up?"

139

"He said she was a gift from some people he'd done work for."

Uncle Doc raised an eyebrow. "And I suppose the people moved away?"

"That's right! How did you know?"

"Oh, at times I'm real bright," the vet declared. He gave Suzy a pat on the rump to let her know she could jump off the table. Then he sank down in the nearest chair and pulled his lower lip with his thumb and index finger, still considering the dog as she trotted around to stand beside Jo.

"Shortridge gait too," he muttered. "Springy. I can generally spot 'em."

"You mean—?" Jo prompted him.

"I mean she could be a Shortridge dog. I'm not saying she is, but she could be. All the points."

"Shortridge?"

"Heavens, child, didn't you ever hear of the Shortridge Kennels? They're up beyond Valley Forge, off the Phoenixville road. Norman Shortridge has been breeding beagles ever since he inherited old J. G.'s fortune. Good ones too."

"You mean valuable?"

"Bet your life."

Jo felt as if she had been placed, to borrow an expression from her mother, between the devil and the deep-blue sea. If the beagle should be a Shortridge dog who somehow had fallen into Howard Land's hands, Suzy would be returned to the impersonal comfort of a gentleman's kennel and be taught to run with a pack. But she would go out of Jo's life, nevertheless. And for the first

140

time Jo realized that this was what she was really fighting. She didn't want to give Suzy up!

Momentarily Jo closed her eyes. Oh, if only she had stifled the impulse to place that ad!

She returned to reality to hear Uncle Doc saying, "Tell you what. I've got to take a run up to the Shortridge farm tomorrow, and I'll just tote Suzy along. Norman Shortridge can identify her quick enough if she's one of his dogs. She'd be out of a late fall litter, like as not."

"But what am I going to tell Mr. Land?" Jo asked.

"You tell him I've got the pup and he can see me," Dr. Webster said promptly.

"Tomorrow's Saturday." Jo was only thinking that a weekend might postpone action.

But Uncle Doc missed the point. "It's still a working day for me," he told her with a rueful chuckle. Suzy had come over and put her paws on his knees, and he was caressing her absently. Then, like a busy man who pushes ahead out of habit, he straightened. "Got a lead, Jo? I might as well take her along now. Save me some time tomorrow."

Reluctantly Jo went to fetch a leash—Inky's red leather one.

"Everything else all right?" Uncle Doc asked when she came back.

"Everything's fine," Jo replied. Then, out of courtesy, she asked, "Want to see the dogs?"

"Not tonight. I've got an operation to do. I'll look them over when I bring this pooch back. If I bring her back," he corrected himself.

Jo's chest felt hot, and there was an area just below her

throat that was stretched taut. Uncle Doc didn't realize what he was saying, what he was doing to her! He thought he was walking off with just another dog, a rabbit hound, a beagle pup, a stray.

As she was led away Suzy kept looking back over her shoulder at Jo, questioning, uncertain. Jo nodded to tell her it was all right, but her lips felt frozen to her teeth. She stood looking after the familiar car, even when she could no longer see Suzy, and tears she didn't bother to brush away began to roll silently down her cheeks.

Except for the day of her father's departure the house had never seemed so empty and comfortless to Jo as it did during the next hour, before her mother's return. Even after Mrs. Redmond bustled into the kitchen, her arms full of packages, there was a peculiar cheerlessness. Something was missing, the soft following patter of Suzy Beagle's feet.

Try as she would, she couldn't rouse herself to make conversation during dinner. After the dishes were dried she went out to the garden alone and flopped on the old chaise lounge that had been her father's favorite resting-place. She lay on her stomach, her cheek against the cracked green covering of simulated leather, and pulled at tufts of grass with the fingers of one hand.

She didn't know how long she stayed there without changing position. She felt tense and unwilling to move, as though any gesture might push her over the brink of disaster. The light on the grass died with the coming of dusk, and the birds were quiet. Even the dogs seemed subdued.

Then a teasing male voice, almost directly above Jo's

142

head, asked, " 'Why so pale and wan, pale lady? Prithee, why so pale?' " Chuck struck an attitude, and added with his usual instinct for clowning, "I quote."

"You misquote," said Jo, hoping she was right. She sat up and ran her fingers through her hair, where it had been mashed flat on the cushion of the chaise. "Hi, Chuck. Sit down. I'm feeling a bit low."

"Me too," replied Chuck promptly. "I smashed a fender on Dad's car and came over here for comfort and cheer. On foot, I might add."

"You never walked?" Jo looked at Chuck's plump, bright-eyed face in pretended consternation. "You'll be fading away to a shadow with all that exercise."

Chuck sighed. "Always belittlin'. I'll have you know it's nearly a mile."

It was a game of words Jo knew by heart, she had played it so many times. Almost without thinking she retorted, "Tch, tch! You'll get bunions." Then she added, with ready sympathy, "Tell me about the car."

"A woman driver," said Chuck sadly, shaking his head.

Jo bridled. "I was reading some statistics the other day. Women drivers have fewer accidents than men."

Chuck snorted. "Statistics!" He shook a finger. "Who compiled 'em, a woman?"

They talked on, nonsense dialogue that eased Jo more than she realized. Her perspective began to return, and she even roused herself to ask, after a while, whether Chuck would like a Coke.

"Have I ever turned down anything for the inner man?"

Jo went into the kitchen to get a bottle and glasses. Her

143

mother, writing a letter in the living room, called from the desk, "Is that Steve out there?"

"No, Chuck. Want a Coke?"

"Thanks, not now."

"I do," called Ricky from the couch, where he was resting on the back of his neck, looking at television.

"Come and get it!" Jo poured an extra glass.

She went back to the lawn carrying a tray, and found another dim masculine form stretched out in a chair next to Chuck's. "Speaking of angels," she said. "Hi, Steve."

"Hi. Any left for me?"

"Plenty. Want me to get you some?"

"I'll get it." Steve ambled up to the house, where Jo could hear him chatting with her mother for several minutes before he came back again. Chuck, on his way to the kitchen for a refill, passed him en route.

"I can't stay," Steve said almost at once, although Jo noticed that he sat down again as if he had nowhere in particular to go. "When I stopped by this afternoon I forgot something. I meant to ask you whether you'd like to go swimming at the Mill Pond tomorrow afternoon. I'm invited to a brunch and I'm allowed to bring a girl."

He produced the invitation in a rush, as though he wanted to get things settled while Chuck was out of hearing. It occurred to Jo that perhaps Steve thought he was cutting in on Chuck's time, and she could scarcely conceal her amusement, which was almost as great as her surprise.

"Why, that would be very nice, Stephen," she said sedately. "I'd enjoy it. What time?"

14

MAYBE IT WAS because the kitchen door banged behind Chuck just as Steve replied. Maybe it was because Jo's mind was still on Suzy and she wasn't really paying attention. She never knew, later, how she had happened to get the time confused, but she was definitely under the impression that Steve had told her he would stop by for her at one o'clock. Instead, he showed up at twelve fifteen.

Jo, still in jeans and an old work shirt, was lying on top of the sloping roof of Roger's sleeping quarters when he arrived.

Ricky, who had been sent back to the house to fetch some nails, greeted him. "How come you aren't working today?" he asked. "I thought you had a job at Brett's."

"I get every other Saturday afternoon off," Steve told him.

Ricky, who was feeling put upon because Jo was becoming edgy over the stubborn length of wire with which she was trying to roof Roger's pen, muttered, "H'm. Pretty soft."

"Want to trade?"

"Didja ever try to work for my sister?"

Steve laughed. "Where is Jo? Dressing?"

Ricky wagged a thumb in the direction of the kennels. "Nope. She's back there struggling with a coil of wire some guy handed her for free."

Steve laughed again. "I'm the guy," he told Ricky. "I'll go see what's up."

"You'll prob'bly get your head bitten off." Ricky continued on his errand to the house.

For a few seconds Steve, unseen, stood and watched Jo trying to pin down the obstinate chicken wire. Her forehead was streaked with dirt, and perspiration glistened on her upper lip, but her hair was bright and soft around her face, damp where it curled close to her ears. She drove a double-headed tack into one of the posts with a hammer, hit her finger and started to suck it. "Darn!"

Then she glanced up and saw Steve.

"What are you doing here?"

"I thought we were going to a party."

"At one o'clock, wasn't it?"

"At twelve fifteen."

Jo sighed. "Really? I'm awfully sorry. I'll let this wire go and be ready in ten minutes." She looked harassed.

Steve said, "There's no mad chase." He stepped forward. "Mind if I offer a suggestion? You're doing that all wrong."

Jo bit her lip to keep from making a snappy reply, but Steve apparently hadn't meant to offend her. "Those tacks are going to rust," he continued, "and they'll be the dickens to get out. Do you suppose your dad has a coil

146

of pliable wire anywhere around?"

Ricky, returning, overheard. "I know where there's one. In the garage."

"Will you get it?" Steve asked, taking charge.

"This should do the trick." He nodded when he had the wire in his hands. "Look. Let's thread it through the wire netting and then wind it around the corner posts. Like this." He demonstrated while Jo and Ricky looked on. Then he turned to the boy. "Think you could do it?"

The question was a challenge. "Sure."

"Okay. You take over while Jo changes her clothes. I'll help if you need me."

"I won't need you," said Ricky with solid decisiveness. "You just run along and play."

Scrambling down from the roof, Jo turned to wrinkle her nose in amusement, but she made no comment. Ricky was doing quite a job around the place these days. She hurried up to the house, changed into a cotton dress and sandals, then came back to the kennel yard in search of Steve.

He was standing in front of Bitsy's pen looking contemplative, and her brother was working away with a will, lacing the pliable wire thread through the fence and the new mesh roof of Roger's domain.

"Ready?" Jo called.

Steve turned, then whistled in admiration. "Pretty sharp."

"Thanks." Jo dropped a mock curtsy, and Ricky snorted eloquently.

"Say, Jo," Steve asked, "is there anything wrong with this cocker? She just lies here and pants."

147

"It's the heat," Jo said. "Besides which, she gobbles her food." She pushed away any concern except that which she felt for Suzy. Remembering something, she turned to Ricky. "If Mr. Land should show up, tell him he's to see Dr. Webster about the beagle, will you?"

"Sure. When are you getting home?"

Jo turned to Steve, questioning.

"About four."

"Okay. Mom's going to be out, and I want to go swimming when you get here, so don't let me down."

"We won't," promised Steve, man to man.

The picnic lunch at the Mill Pond Club was well under way when Jo and Steve arrived, but there was plenty of food and several mutual friends, among them Nancy Valentine and Bill Hamilton. The crowd loafed around the edge of the pool for an hour after lunch, sunbathing, then swam when the water was warmest, in midafternoon.

It was exactly four o'clock when Steve and Jo arrived home. All along the way Jo had felt her impatience increasing. By now Uncle Doc might have phoned about Suzy. She could scarcely wait to reach the house.

But when she questioned Ricky, who was sitting down by the mailbox with his swimming trunks and towel under his arm, ready and waiting for the chance to dash off to Martin's Dam, Jo learned that the telephone had been abnormally quiet.

"Uncle Doc hasn't called?"

"Nope. Nobody's called." Ricky was already on his way down the road. "But there's something wrong with Bitsy. She's been yelling like crazy for the last couple of hours."

148

"What do you mean, yelling?" Jo called after him.

"Sort of crying. Not all the time. Just now and then. As though she had a bad pain."

Jo sighed and said to Steve, "I guess I'd better take a look at her." Why did it always have to be cocker spaniels that claimed her attention, when her chief concern was for Suzy Beagle and her undecided fate?

Hands in his pockets, and whistling idly, Steve followed her back to the kennels. Ricky had been right. Bitsy was literally howling. Jo could hear her even before she passed the hedge.

"Golly," she wondered aloud, "what can be wrong?"

The wirehaired terrier who occupied the adjoining pen was sitting on his haunches eyeing the cocker curiously. All the dogs set up a racket as Steve, a stranger, appeared, but Jo quieted them with a firm command.

Bitsy was crouched against the board front of the long kennel house. She had dug herself a hole in the earth and was turning and turning as if she was making a nest, shivering and whimpering alternately.

Jo opened the gate and ducked inside the enclosure to crouch and try to comfort her with reassuring words and gentle stroking. Steve followed, squatting on the balls of his feet at Jo's side.

His eyebrows drew together as he watched Bitsy silently. Then he said, as calmly as though he were passing the time of day, "I can tell you what's wrong with this dog, Jo. She's about to have pups."

"Pups?" Jo looked up at him in utter astonishment. "Bitsy?"

Steve nodded. "Sure. When did Dr. Webster see her last?"

Jo tried to think. "He hasn't really looked at the dogs for weeks now. Except the ones that needed attention, I mean."

"That explains it," Steve conceded. "But what about Bitsy's owners? Didn't they say anything?"

Jo shook her head. "I guess they didn't know."

She looked down at the cocker again in puzzled alarm. "I'd better phone Uncle Doc right away. I wouldn't have the slightest idea in the world what to do."

"I'd get her a little more comfortable," suggested Steve. "How about an old cardboard carton and some shredded newspapers and a clean piece of blanket or a worn-out sheet?"

"I'll see what I can find."

"Bring them back here. I don't think we're going to have too much time."

"Maybe it would be better to move her up to the house," suggested Jo. But Steve shook his head. "These quarters are familiar to her. She'll be happier here for the time being."

As Jo ran to do the errands Steve had prompted she continued to be amazed at his calmness and common sense.

She assembled the newspapers and a torn piece of soft, clean sheeting and took them along with a big cardboard carton back to Bitsy's pen. Steve had already brought the terrified cocker fresh drinking water, which she lapped thirstily.

"Now I'll go call Uncle Doc."

Steve nodded. "She'll probably be able to manage things by herself," he said reassuringly. "But she's so scared that I'll bet this is her first litter."

Jo shook her head. "I wouldn't know."

Still crouching on the ground, Steve was shredding newspapers and fluffing them in the bottom of the box. "If things are normal, she'll be fine," he said as he worked. "But I understand that forceps whelping is quite common these days, especially with city dogs and house pets." He picked up the sheeting and folded it on top of his bedding base.

Jo stopped in undisguised surprise.

"How do you get to know things like that?"

"Oh, I read a little, now and then." Steve grinned and shrugged. "I probably read more than you do, Mrs. Truck!"

Jo pondered this statement as she hurried back to the house. She was aware that he had been teasing, but remembered that Steve had wanted to be a doctor, that obstetrics probably interested him. She picked up the telephone and dialed Dr. Webster's number hurriedly.

For an endless time there was no answer. Then Mrs. Webster's pleasant, throaty voice said, "Hello."

"Mrs. Webster? This is Jo Redmond. Is Uncle Doc home?"

"Oh, hello, Josie! No. He went up to the Shortridge place with that beagle of yours."

"Do you suppose I can reach him there?"

"You can try. He had some other calls to make,

though. Is anything wrong?"

"Yes," Jo confessed. "Sort of. I think one of my boarders is going to have pups."

Mrs. Webster laughed. "Really? Right this minute?"

"Well, practically!"

The veterinarian's wife sobered. "What breed?"

"Cocker spaniel."

Mrs. Webster hesitated. "She probably won't have any trouble, but I do think Luke would like to be alerted, just in case. Try him at the Shortridge Kennels, Jo, and if you can't reach him there, I'll give him your message as soon as he gets home. And, Jo—"

"Yes?"

"Just make the mother as comfortable as possible and let her take charge. You'll be amazed at the efficient job she'll do. The puppies will probably come at intervals of about half an hour, once the whelping starts. And when it seems to be over, move the mother gently to a clean bed and give her a little warm milk to drink. No food."

Jo gulped. "All right. And thanks a lot."

Her fingers trembled as she flipped through the pages of the telephone directory looking for the number of the Shortridge Kennels. When she found it and dialed, a male voice answered with a gruff "hello."

"Hello. Is Doctor Webster there?"

"Doc Webster? He was here, but he left about half an hour ago."

"You—you wouldn't know where I could reach him?"

"No, I wouldn't, miss."

"All right. Thank you." Jo hung up.

The kitchen clock showed that she had spent fifteen

minutes on the two telephone calls. She went out to the kennel hesitantly, repeating in her mind Mrs. Webster's advice—*The puppies will probably come at half-hour intervals.*

Steve was still crouched near Bitsy's improvised bed. His back was to Jo, but he turned at the sound of her approach and put a finger to his lips. "Come here!"

Jo stooped to duck through the kennel gate. She could see at once that Bitsy was quieter now, although she was still panting. Then the spaniel bent her head quickly and licked at something, and Jo gasped as she realized that it was a small, taffy-colored, newborn puppy tumbling helplessly about under its mother's cleansing tongue.

"It's only three minutes old," Steve whispered. "Isn't it big!"

Very quietly, so that she wouldn't disturb Bitsy, Jo knelt by the box.

"Big? Why, it's the tiniest thing I've ever seen!" Jo whispered back, but she began to understand the wonder in Steve's eyes. The little creature with its tight-shut eyes seemed miraculous to her too.

It had a head far too big for its feeble body, and a snout like a baby pig. The mouth was disproportionately large and searching, and minute toenails were visible on its pink, hairless feet. The ears, instead of being long and feathery, like Bitsy's, were very odd. They lay back flat against the puppy's head, like miniature canoe paddles, dark gray and rubbery.

But it was alive! It was already making an instinctive sucking motion with its hungry mouth. It was alive, and it was silky and as sleek as wet plush.

153

"Isn't it wonderful!"

The awe in Steve's voice was completely sincere, and Jo nodded without speaking. It didn't seem upsetting now, as it had a few minutes ago, that she and Steve should together be officiating at Bitsy's accouchement. She was glad Steve was here. He was a comfort and, in case of emergency, he might prove to be a help.

"I couldn't reach Uncle Doc," Jo remembered to report, "but Mrs. Webster says she'll tell him as soon as he gets home. She says the puppies will come about every half hour. I imagine we could leave Bitsy alone now if you like."

But Steve shook his head. "She might roll on this one and smother it." He glanced across at Jo. "You go on if you have things to do. I'll stay here."

15

THREE PUPPIES were born before six o'clock. From the moment the first puppy arrived Bitsy stopped shivering. Nor did she whimper at the advent of successive members of her new family. Her eyes looked larger and more intelligent than ever before, and Jo could scarcely believe that the high-strung cocker had changed so abruptly to the epitome of maternal efficiency.

Unobtrusively Steve kept watch. The firstborn pup began to push itself around on its tiny legs, nuzzling the mother for milk, and when she nosed it aside to attend to the more important needs of a new arrival, the baby opened his curved mouth and protested with a squeal.

"For all the world like a baby chick cheeping," said Steve to Jo, who was going about the necessary business of feeding the rest of her boarding dogs. "Just listen to that!"

Mrs. Redmond arrived home just as Bitsy was giving her third pup its introductory bath. "Invite me to dinner, won't you, please?" Steve asked with unexpected boldness. "I wouldn't miss this for anything. And could I ask you to phone my mother and tell her why I won't be home. She'll understand.''

Jo had seldom heard Steve speak of his family, although she had a nodding acquaintance with both his parents, and when her own mother returned to the house to phone Mrs. Chance and start preparations for supper, she looked at him quizzically. "What did you mean by that? Saying your mother would understand?''

"You'd have to know her, Jo. She's a lot like me. Always hankered to be a doctor, or at least a nurse, when she was young.''

Then, as though he had admitted too much, he changed the subject abruptly. "I'll make a bet with you.''

"Yes?''

"I'll bet this is the last in the litter. Aren't first litters often small? That would account for the fact that Bitsy's condition went undetected, wouldn't it?''

"Even your phraseology is getting clinical,'' Jo teased him. "Would it, Doctor Chance?''

For the first time in her memory, Jo saw Steve blush. He turned away from her and bent over Bitsy, risking the gesture of picking up one of her puppies to examine it at close range. The cocker started to growl, then apparently decided she could trust Steve, and changed her mind. Jo moved closer to touch the smooth back of the round-headed creature which lay like a fat mole in Steve's palm. "They are pretty remarkable, aren't they?''

The boy nodded. "Here's your baby back,'' he told Bitsy. "See, I didn't hurt her.'' But Bitsy nevertheless washed the puppy all over again.

Jo was going back to the house to warm some milk for

the new mother when Uncle Doc's car turned into the lane. She changed her course and ran across the lawn anxiously, straining to see whether Suzy was in the seat beside him.

For several seconds her heart stood still. There was no sign of the beagle. Then Uncle Doc opened the door on the far side of the car and Suzy raced around the front wheels to hurl herself like a catapult on Jo.

"Suzy! Suzy Beagle!" Sinking to her knees, Jo gathered the ecstatic dog into her arms, and looked up at Uncle Doc hopefully.

The gravity of his expression stifled her joy. Don't count your chickens before they're hatched, his eyes seemed to say. Jo got to her feet and waited.

The veterinarian pushed his hat back on his head, and pulled the lobe of one ear thoughtfully. "Darnedest mix-up you ever heard of, Jo. This pup doesn't belong to Land, but I found out who she does belong to."

Jo swallowed hard. "Who?"

"Some people in Ardmore by the name of Lyon." Dr. Webster took Jo's arm and propelled her toward the back of the house as he talked. "It seems this Mrs. Lyon won Suzy on a twenty-five-cent chance at the Devon Horse Show last spring. You know how people donate every-thing from cars to puppies to be raffled off for the benefit of Bryn Mawr Hospital? Well, Norm Shortridge crashed through with this pup and a highfalutin pedigree. She was so cute and appealing she walked away with two hun-dred and fifty dollars in twenty-five-cent chances, and Mrs. Lyon won. You following me?"

Jo nodded. "Yes."

"We tried to get the Lyons on the telephone from up at the farm, but there was no answer. It looks as though the beagle was either stolen or just plain got lost. In any event, I decided it was horse sense to bring her back here and let you get in touch with the Lyons tomorrow or whenever they turn up at home. Maybe you can make a dicker with 'em for her board and keep, so that you won't be out of pocket for your expenses."

As though that mattered. As though that mattered at all! But Jo knew Dr. Webster was only trying to guard her interests and make a businesslike approach to the problem. He couldn't possibly guess how deeply attached she had become to the hound.

And Jo found that she couldn't tell him.

"How much is a beagle pup like Suzy worth?" she asked on impulse.

Uncle Doc pursed his lips. "Oh, I'd say somewhere around a hundred dollars."

It was too much for Jo. There wasn't that much money in her bank account yet, though by the end of the summer she should have earned double or triple that amount. Even so, it could not be used for the luxury of buying a dog. That money was to go toward her tuition and board in college.

It was apparently inevitable that she would lose Suzy, and she tried to comfort herself with the thought that at least it wouldn't be to Mr. Land. "I wonder where Howard Land comes into the picture?" she asked of Uncle Doc. "Suzy recognized him. I'm sure of that. She was scared of him, too."

"I'll take care of Land," Uncle Doc promised. "He

may have picked her up along the road somewhere. Probably didn't steal her, just appropriated her when he found she was lost, and kept her tied up."

"He hasn't shown up yet today."

Uncle Doc shrugged. "Maybe he never will." He added, "But if he should, just send him to me, the way I told you." Then he changed the subject as they came within sight of the kennels. "What about this cocker you phoned about? Helen said you had an idea she might be going to whelp."

"Might be?" Jo laughed spontaneously. "She has."

"Well, for Pete's sake!" Uncle Doc looked astonished. "That's one on me. I should have spotted her last time I looked over the kennels. But sometimes you get 'em like that. No visual change at all until three or four days before whelping time. I'll wager her owners will be plenty surprised!"

"I'll bet they will too," Jo conceded, trying to let the talk about Bitsy take her mind off the beagle. As they started down the path, Steve was just ducking through the gate of the cocker's pen. He straightened when he saw Dr. Webster and said, "How do you do, sir."

"This is Stephen Chance, Uncle Doc. He's been more help than a trained nurse."

Dr. Webster, grinning, held out his hand. "How do you like playing vet, Stephen?"

"It was mighty interesting, sir."

"Any trouble?"

"None at all."

Uncle Doc nodded. "Good. Nine times out of ten, things go all right."

"And the tenth time?"

The veterinarian shrugged. "Due to civilization, I suppose, and the soft life, Cesarean operations are getting quite common. Especially with apartment house pets."

"I'd like to watch a Cesarean sometime, Dr. Webster," Steve said.

Uncle Doc considered Steve quizzically. "We'll talk about it. Now I'd better take a look, as long as I'm here."

"Are the puppies going to be cockers, Uncle Doc, or mongrels?" Jo asked. "Or can't you tell yet?"

"I can tell." The doctor, after he had quieted Bitsy's fear that he might harm her babies, examined each of the three pups in turn. "They'll be cockers all right," he assured Jo. "Two dogs and one bitch. A nice litter. Fat as pigs, aren't they?"

"The third one was born about forty-five minutes ago," Steve told the vet. "She doesn't act as if she's going to have any more."

"No, I think that's the last," Dr. Webster agreed after a minute. "Well, you kids have taken this pretty calmly."

"It was Steve who was calm, not me," Jo confessed. "If he hadn't been here, I'd have been scared."

"A pretty little speech, Josie," laughed Uncle Doc as he came through the kennel gate and shut it after him. "But even alone, you'd have come through all right. You're not as helpless as you pretend to be."

Steve's eyes met Dr. Webster's, and now it was Jo's turn to blush. She could feel the unbecoming red creeping up her neck. Chin in the air, she turned and started back toward the house, missing Uncle Doc's knowing wink.

"I'd leave the new mother alone for another hour or so. Then I'd move her and her brood into the kitchen for the next couple of weeks," Dr. Webster suggested before he left. "She'll be happier away from the other dogs."

He gave Jo instructions about feeding a nursing mother, stopped to say hello to Mrs. Redmond and to caution Ricky to approach Bitsy with care. "Better not touch the pups at all for a few days, fella. Bitsy's got responsibilities, and she might just lash out and take a piece out of your hand."

As though he felt thoroughly at home, Steve helped clear the table after dinner, and even managed to coax Ricky into an assembly line for the dishwashing job. Then Jo and the boys moved Bitsy and her family to the house, made them comfortable in a corner of the kitchen, and closed the door against the possible intrusion of Suzy, who would surely be unwelcome for the next few days.

After Ricky went off to bed, Jo and Steve put some country music on the record player and sat out on the front steps in the moonlight, listening to the spirited tunes. They didn't talk much, just sat there, and between them lay Suzy Beagle, her head in Jo's lap.

If only tomorrow would never come, Jo kept thinking —if only I didn't have to call the Lyons, I'd be perfectly happy tonight!

16

THAT NIGHT SUZY BEAGLE slept on the rug once occupied by Roger, at the foot of Jo's bed, and if Jo leaned over the side, she could see the little dog lying there in the moonlight, utterly contented and relaxed, her belly and throat and four white paws visible in the darkness.

The next morning Jo was awakened by Suzy's tongue brushing her cheek like wet silk. She opened her eyes and stretched out a hand languidly. The beagle's forepaws were on the bed, her tail was wagging, and her eyes pleaded for an invitation she knew would come.

"Suzy!"

The word was enough. Suzy's head was wriggling into the curve of Jo's neck, and she settled down happily. Then Jo remembered she had to call the Lyons. With Suzy warm in her arms she began to search for ways to procrastinate. Church! She would wait until after church.

Later in the morning Jo was grateful for the chores that kept her moving. The usual kennel routine—pens to be cleaned, fresh water to be distributed, Bitsy and her brood to be given special attention. At twelve thirty, when her conscience began to tickle, Steve stopped by to see if the pups were doing all right, and Jo let this serve as an excuse for further delay.

"I have a tennis date with Chuck," he told her. "Want to come along? We'll have some mixed doubles if we can find another girl."

"I'll call Ginny," Jo suggested, and deliberately ignored the Lyons' number scrawled on the telephone pad. Ginny said, "Sure, I'll play some tennis. Meet you at the club?" and Jo changed into sneakers and a short white tennis dress. She continued to ignore the number on the telephone pad when she ran downstairs, but Steve, holding the screen door for her, asked bluntly, "Have you connected with the owners of the beagle yet?"

"Not yet."

"Have you tried to reach them?" Steve prodded.

Jo frowned. "No, I haven't. I've been busy."

"What's the matter with now?" Steve paused on the steps. "There's no mad rush to get to the club."

"There's no mad rush to call the Lyons either. They'll keep."

Steve shook his head. "I can't understand getting steamed up about a stray dog."

Instantly on the defensive, Jo retorted, "You were pretty steamed up about Bitsy and her pups yesterday afternoon. And you were interested enough to stop by to see how they were getting along today."

"Sure. Sure," Steve admitted. "I'm interested, but my emotions aren't involved. You know what I was thinking, last evening? I was thinking it was a great waste of talent for Doc Webster to have been a vet, when he could have been a doctor. When he could have spent his life taking care of people, not animals. When he could have done something really worthwhile!"

Jo, who was getting into the car, slammed the door violently. "If that isn't the most narrow-minded speech I've ever heard!" she spluttered indignantly.

Steve looked surprised. "Why? I'm not criticizing Doctor Webster as a person. Anybody can see he's a fine man. I just don't understand his point of view."

"Of course you don't!" Jo agreed. "Any more than you understand mine. You ought to come down to earth once in a while."

"You'd better explain yourself," Steve said. He hadn't started the motor.

Jo wondered whether she could explain herself. "I remember something my dad said once. When he got out of school he was a lot like you, I guess. Full of big ideas. Nothing but the best would do for him! He wanted to go into international banking. It sounded pretty glamorous and exciting, he said. It was the tops. And where did he end up? As a small-town banker. He laughed at himself when he told me about it, but he said, 'It's good for kids to dream, Jo. But it's also important for them to be able to make an adjustment to everyday life.' "

Steve's expression was puzzled. "What's that got to do with me?"

Jo took a long breath. "Don't you see? You're a lot like my dad was. You think big. You want to be a doctor—or you did. But with you it's all or nothing. You're stymied because you can't see where the money is coming from —the money it would take to study medicine. You're scared to start for fear you might have to stop. Isn't that it?"

For a moment Jo was afraid she had gone too far. Steve's eyes darkened and narrowed. His lips thinned. Then, unexpectedly, he shrugged and admitted, "That's about it."

"I think you ought to go ahead regardless," Jo told him firmly. "Take a premed course in college. If you don't get to medical school, so what? You'll be a laboratory worker, perhaps, or a chemist. Or maybe, if you're good enough, you'll get a scholarship and somehow or other you'll make your dream come true."

Steve didn't answer. He started the car, backed down the drive, and swung into the road, accelerating. "It seems to me we've gotten a little off the subject," he said after a minute. "We were discussing Doctor Webster's feelings for dogs."

"And mine," Jo added. She had already said so much she might as well say everything she had on her mind. "Uncle Doc loves working with animals. He feels warm toward them, the way I do. When they're sick or hurt he wants to help them get better. He's interested in medicine and surgery for horses and cows and dogs the way you're interested in the human body. Don't you see?"

"Not really," said Steve.

Jo turned and tucked her feet under her. "Have you ever had a dog, Steve?" she asked.

Steve shook his head. They were approaching an intersection, and he looked from left to right without meeting Jo's eyes. "My pop never thought much of animals around a house."

Jo sighed in relief. "That explains it."

"Explains what?"

"Explains why you don't understand the way I feel about Suzy Beagle. Explains why you can't get Uncle Doc's point of view. Oh, I wish I could make you see!"

They were approaching the entrance to the tennis club, but Steve ignored it and started to drive on around the block. "You can try," he told Jo. "I'm quite intelligent."

He sounded calm and detached, and that frightened her. This wasn't a question of intelligence. It was a question of emotion. She clasped her hands in her lap and tried to think her feelings into words.

"Steve, look at it this way," she said after a while. "Some people—especially children—need dogs. They need to feel loved, and they need to know the loyalty a dog can give them. Maybe after people grow up and get married and have children, dogs aren't so important to them. I don't know. But I know Suzy Beagle's important to me now, and I know I'm important to her. Really important! Oh, I'm saying this all so badly." Jo stopped.

For a long minute Steve didn't reply. He was driving very slowly, but it wouldn't be long before they reached the entrance drive again. A car turned in ahead of them and Steve followed, edging neatly into a parking space and turning off the ignition key. Then, to Jo's surprise, he reached over and patted her clasped hands.

"You haven't said it badly at all. You've said it rather well. I guess I've been sort of a stinker about the dog business, Jo."

Before Jo could protest, Chuck was at the side of the car. "Hey," he complained. "What's the deal? You drive around the block like you're going to a funeral, and all the time you're fifteen minutes late for our tennis date, Steve. I can't hold a court forever, you know."

"Sorry, fella." Steve reached into the back of the car for the two racquets. "Is Ginny here? I did a switch on you and made it mixed doubles. Okay?"

"Sure, it's okay," said Chuck with returning good humor. "I won't have to run so hard."

Ginny pulled in as he was greeting Jo and the four of them walked over to the courts, shedding their racquet presses and extra balls. They tossed for partners and started to play.

For the first five minutes Jo was badly off her game. Then she straightened out and concentrated, strengthening her serve. She was playing with Chuck, and his clowning lost them some points, but even so they managed to make it a deuce set before Steve and Ginny finally took it away.

They changed partners and played again. Chuck was puffing a little now, but he had stopped his high jinks, and his fast, low returns won Ginny and him the first three games.

"Come on, Jo! We're slipping," Steve urged. "Stop wondering whether you've ruined a beautiful friendship and get those serves over the net!"

"I wasn't—" Jo started, but her essential honesty made her leave the denial incomplete because of course she was worrying about whether she had hurt Steve's feelings.

"Cut out the conversation and play ball!" Chuck was yelling. "What the heck's the matter with you two?"

167

"Ready?" Jo called.

"Serve!"

This one was good, bullet-like and low, right to the center corner of the court. Chuck swung and missed it, inches high. "Hey!" he complained.

Steve tossed Jo the third ball and she stepped back to position again. Somehow, though nothing had been said between them that really counted, she knew that Steve wasn't offended, that everything was going to be all right.

She began to play with surprising zest, and they took the set 6–4. "Want any more?" asked Steve.

Chuck pulled out a handkerchief and wiped his perspiring brow. "Not me, coach!" He sighed. "I'll be glad when I'm too old for sports."

They all walked over to the turf that edged the courts, and sat down behind the facing benches. Ginny started to look for four-leaf clovers in the grass and Chuck helped her. After a few minutes Jane Allen and Nancy Valentine, who had been playing singles, wandered up.

Nancy, looking cool and unruffled as always, squatted on her heels. "Anybody going swimming?" she asked. "We are."

"Will you save me if I sink on the way to the raft?" asked Chuck. "I'm weak as a mink."

The mental portrait of diminutive Nancy towing Chuck to shore made everybody laugh. "I'll lend you my water wings," Ginny promised.

"Aw, gee." Chuck stuck a finger in his mouth.

It was the usual foolish talk, carefree and bubbling. It was just like every other summer. Ginny didn't seem a bit different, nor did Chuck, but Jo felt a restlessness, an urgency, that communicated itself to Steve. He looked up and met her eyes.

Nothing was said but, as on the tennis court, a spark of understanding leaped between them. Jo dropped her glance.

"Gail Chartriss is coming home tomorrow," Ginny was saying.

"Woof, woof!" Chuck did a poor imitation of a wolf.

Gail had seemed important to Jo at the beginning of the summer, but now, on the first of August, she only had a certain nuisance value. Like the chitchat of the crowd, she was superficial. And she had a feeling that Steve would react to her just as she did, now.

It was wonderful, that feeling of confidence, that feeling that she and Steve—together—were moving on. Even their arguments became valuable to her, because everything added up.

"Dandelion fluff," Steve was saying to Chuck. He blew on his fingers. "Gone with the wind."

"What are you talking about?" asked Ginny, frowning, but Jo knew.

She laughed, to cover Steve's failure to reply, and got up. "I don't think I'd better go swimming," she said. "I've got things to do."

"Dogs, dogs, dogs," Ginny pouted.

Steve got to his feet too. "One dog, this time," he corrected her. "Come on, Josie, face the music! We'll go and beard the Lyons in their den."

17

THE LYONS WERE AWAY on vacation. The only person Jo and Steve managed to beard was a sleepy-eyed apartment house superintendent who told them that their quarry was in Cape May and wouldn't be home until the following Saturday night, late.

"Did the Lyons have a little hound dog—a beagle?" Jo asked.

The superintendent scratched the back of his neck. "Yup," he said thoughtfully. "Seems like I remember Mrs. Lyons won a pup in a raffle somewhere. They don't have it now, though."

"No. I know," murmured Jo.

"Just as well. We got a new ruling no dogs is allowed in these apartments."

Jo's heart gave a hopeful leap. "Really?"

The man nodded. "Could be," he said, "that's why the Lyons didn't renew. They're moving, middle of the month."

"Oh." Jo looked stricken. The superintendent couldn't

know what havoc he was wreaking. "Well, thanks, anyway," she said.

On the way home in the car she was sober and quiet. Then, as they left Wayne behind and turned into country roads again, she lifted her head. "Well," she said, "I'll have Suzy Beagle for one more week, and in a week anything can happen."

"You bet," said Steve with some conviction. "It has."

The week that followed, however, was without the drama of the past fortnight. There were no searches in the night, no accouchements among Jo's boarders. There was plenty of work, however, even though it was routine. More and more frequently, when the phone rang it was for Jo, and she managed to book her kennel almost to capacity for August, while the record of deposits in her new bankbook swelled appreciably. With far more self-confidence than she had shown a month before, she welcomed new boarders and returned seasoned ones.

Of Trinket, the poodle, she was especially proud. Trinket had definitely gained in personality during her weeks in the kennel. Even Mrs. Chartriss recognized it.

She called the Redmond house three days after her return from Maine and asked to speak to Josephine. "I don't know what you've done to our poodle, but she acts like a different dog. She's lost all her nervousness, and she seems three times as intelligent. We're quite impressed!"

Jo almost made a brusque reply. She didn't like or admire Mrs. Chartriss, but she remembered, in time, that her loyalty to the dog outweighed this. "Trinket is quite a remarkable dog, Mrs. Chartriss," she replied smoothly.

"She needs lots of understanding and affection, but she responds more quickly than any dog I've ever known."

"Really?" trilled Mrs. Chartriss on the other end of the wire. Jo could tell that she was the sort of woman who, in cars or jewels or houses or dogs, was always flattered when someone admitted she had the best.

"I think Trinket has the makings of a very fine dog," Jo told her.

Roger's owners were also very appreciative of the condition in which he was returned. Jo didn't confess that he had given her one night of anxiety. It was better to let bygones be bygones, she felt, so long as no harm had come to the Great Dane. She received a courteous, friendly note from Mrs. Peter McCallum thanking her for the splendid care Roger had received and sent it on to her dad, proud that she had such a satisfied client.

All week Suzy never left Jo's heels. She was so gentle and quiet that Bitsy even allowed her to come into her corner of the kitchen when Jo attended to the pups.

The litter was certainly thriving! Day by day the three puppies gained weight and strength and lovableness. Two were red-blond and one was black, and all were fat as butter. "No wonder!" commented Jo to her mother. "They nurse all the time."

She never tired of sitting on the floor before Bitsy's box, watching them. Their coats lengthened and acquired a wave, and their bare, ratlike feet became covered with soft down. Bitsy was very solicitous for the first few days, washing them endlessly and never leaving the box for more than a few minutes at a time, but as they grew older she became almost nonchalant in her care of them. Deaf to their squeals, she would desert them whenever she chose, but Jo noticed she was always alert for possible danger, and if a stranger entered the house or a delivery truck pulled into the drive she was back in a flash, stepping into the box so carefully that she never trod on a single paw.

Ricky was equally fascinated by the puppies, but he was more impatient than his sister. "I wish they'd open their eyes! When do they open their eyes?"

"On the ninth day," Jo quoted Uncle Doc.

"All at once—pop!—do they fly open?" Ricky wanted to know.

But Jo couldn't give him any details.

When Dr. Webster stopped by on his weekly visit to the kennels, Jo took him into the kitchen first, to admire Bitsy's brood.

"Golly Ned, they are big!" he said in surprise, picking up one fat, wriggling body. "How old are they? Five days?"

After the puppy had been put back with his mother, Uncle Doc walked back to the kennels with Jo, Suzy Beagle trailing along behind.

"Connect with the Lyons yet?"

"Not yet. They'll be home Sunday," Jo replied, going into no detail.

Uncle Doc nodded, without saying anything banal about wishing her luck. "Now let me see that terrier who's off his feed."

He watched Jo carefully as she handled the wirehaired

terrier, a collie, and the Chesapeake in turn. Each dog seemed to respond to her, to behave calmly under her hand.

"You really get a great kick out of this business, don't you, Jo?" he asked after a while, regarding the girl intently.

"I love dogs," Jo said simply, and smiled.

"Ever think of being a vet?"

"Do women make good veterinarians?"

"Sure. There were four girls in my class at Penn, all very competent."

Laughter suddenly bubbled in Jo's throat. "Wait till I tell Steve Chance!"

Dr. Webster looked puzzled. "I don't get it."

"Steve doesn't have much time for my dog business," Jo started to explain.

"Doesn't he, though!" Uncle Doc cut in. "I called that young fella in on an emergency last night. I tried to reach you first, Jo, but your line was busy and stayed busy for half an hour."

"Ricky," groaned Jo, "talking to Toby Apple."

"It was a ticklish operation," Dr. Webster continued single-mindedly, "and I never saw a more curious mind nor a quicker hand. I'd bet dollars to doughnuts he'll make a surgeon someday."

"Did you tell him so?" asked Jo quickly.

"I did!"

"Good."

"And don't you let him give you any guff about dogs not being important. He's got to learn to love something bad enough. That's all that's wrong with him. He's devel-

174

oped along some lines, like clinical interest, but not along others. There's time. He's young yet."

"If he could only have a dog of his own," Jo mused aloud. "He's never had one in his whole life. Isn't that awful, Uncle Doc?"

Luke Webster looked at Jo through shrewd, narrowed eyes. "Could be he'll get himself a girl, and that'll do the trick just as well," he told her, then turned away quickly so that she wouldn't be embarrassed.

Each night during that short first week of August, Suzy Beagle slept beside Jo's bed, and each night Jo looked at the small calendar on her desk with growing dismay. She wasn't sure she could gather the courage to phone the Lyons.

But at noon on Sunday, Steve came over to see Bitsy's puppies and to drive her, once more, down to Ardmore. "Might as well take the beagle along and get the agony over with," he said. His voice was matter-of-fact, but his eyes were sympathetic as he looked from Jo to Suzy. "Come on! Let's go."

The Lyons were home this time, and answered the buzzer at once. Trying to shout her errand into the mouthpiece of the speaker was far from satisfactory. "Who?" Mr. Lyon kept asking. "What?" Finally he seemed to get a glimmer of what it was all about. "You'd better come up," he said, and pushed the button that opened the main door.

Suzy trotted through the halls and up the stairs obediently enough, but without any show of recognition. Jo's spirits hit rock bottom as she neared the Lyons' open door.

Jo managed to introduce herself and Steve to a middle-aged couple who looked as though the advent of a daughter was a bit too much for them to handle. The child, playing around the rumpled living room, ran over to Suzy at once, shouting, "Goggie, goggie!" and started to pull her ears.

Mrs. Lyon, a dish towel in her hand, said, "Don't do that, dear," to no effect, then admitted that of course the beagle had been their dog, and asked Jo where she had picked her up.

Gradually the entire story was told, both sides of it. The Lyons, driving to Wayne to inspect a house advertised for sale, had left both the beagle and their two-and-a-half-year-old daughter in the car. When they returned, the beagle was gone, and whether the puppy had been stolen or whether she had jumped out the open window they never knew.

"Didn't you get in touch with the police or advertise?" Jo asked.

"I never thought of it," said Mrs. Lyon, looking wide-eyed and incompetent.

"To tell you the truth, we were both a little relieved to be rid of the dog," added Mr. Lyon.

Jo gasped. "Relieved!"

"Well, you see, it was a little difficult—a puppy in an apartment. And the baby and all."

Jo's heart began to pump so fast she thought it must be obvious to all of them. "You—you know there's a new ruling here, that no dogs are allowed?"

"Really?" Mrs. Lyon looked from the beagle to her

husband in unconcealed dismay. "What are we going to do?"

As Jo tried to decide how small a sum she could decently offer for Suzy, Steve stepped in. "I'll tell you what, Mr. Lyon," he said, "If the return of this dog is really going to prove a great inconvenience, we could arrange to take her off your hands."

Mrs. Lyon interceded, voluble with appreciation. "Oh, could you?" she asked. "It would be the greatest help. Because it will be three weeks, more or less, before we'll be able to move."

Steve faced her, straight and tall. "I mean permanently."

"Oh, yes, I mean permanently too. That's quite all right, quite all right with us. Isn't it, dear?"

Mr. Lyon hesitated only a moment, but Steve used that moment to mention, "Of course Suzy has been quite an expense over these past weeks."

The master of the household looked trapped. "I'm afraid we couldn't afford—"

Jo shot a withering glance at Steve. "Of course I wouldn't allow you to pay me anything."

"But we could have the papers, I suppose?" Steve cut in with more perspicacity than Jo dreamed he possessed.

"Papers?"

"The pedigree and the litter registration."

"Oh, yes!" Mrs. Lyon began to fumble in a drawer of the secretary desk. "They're here somewhere."

A few minutes later, unbelievably, Jo and Steve were running down the stairs, Suzy scampering ahead of them.

They were scarcely able to stifle their pent-up laughter until they reached the haven of Steve's car.

"Oh!" Steve leaned back against the seat and roared. "Oh, oh, oh!" He held his sides. "Did you ever see anything so funny as the expression on that man's face?"

But Jo, although she laughed companionably, was primarily aware of a flooding sense of relief. She held Suzy Beagle in her lap, her arms tight around her, and through her summer dress she could feel the little hound's heartbeat.

"She's my girl," she murmured softly into Suzy's ear. Then to Steve she said, "You can't take twenty dogs on a date, but could we occasionally settle for one?"